Cured by Fire

Cured by Fire

TIM MCLAURIN

DOWN HOME

Down Home Press, Asheboro, N.C.

First Paperback Printing—August, 1997
1 2 3 4 5 6 7 8 9

Published by arrangement with G.P. Putnam's Sons, New York

ISBN 1-878086-59-6

Library of Congress Catalog Card Number 97-068984

Printed in the United States of America

The text of this book is set in Caslon.

Cover art by Gary Hawkins
Cover design by Tim Rickard
Book design by MaryJane DiMassi

Down Home Press
P.O. Box 4126
Asheboro, N.C. 27204

This is a story about the bonds between people, about friendship and trust. It is also about conflict and adversity, and about choosing either to stand alone or to clasp hands with another.

I would like to thank the following people, who directly contributed to this book with handshakes and hugs, beers and hard talk, and ties of the human spirit: Faith Sale, Donnalee Frega, Anna Jardine, Jake Mills, Clyde Edgerton, George Terll, Rhoda Weyr, and Gail Chesson.

To Meghan Margaret McLaurin,
my daughter and firstborn

Child-teacher, in our decade as family, I have learned
much of life and love. More easily might I hold all
the stars in my palm than describe the countless rooms
in a father's heart.

God, the great puppeteer, kindly allows us
to pull our own strings,
choosing whom to tug back from disaster's edge.

This is the great question—

That if we dance wildly across the stage
closer to the flames of rage,
will he pull us back,
or let us smolder
in the embers of our self-made blaze.

Debbie Hutchinson, from *Legacy of Storms*

Cured by Fire

BENEATH THE SPANGLED DOME of the night heavens, Lewis Calhoon marched with slow, measured steps up the hillside. The small man he carried was wrapped in a blanket and cradled in his arms like a child. Lewis listened to Elbridge's ragged breath and looked straight ahead, stepping over rocks and rotten logs, skirting trees, his path illuminated by the ivory glow of the full moon. The air was cool on his face; he exhaled in puffs of white vapor. He hitched Elbridge higher in his arms as he strode uphill toward the mountains.

Lewis stopped occasionally and turned to look at the dim windows of the hospital to keep his bearings. A hundred times he had stood on the second-floor balcony to breathe in the cool, fresh air that didn't smell of bandages and disinfectant and vomit, and had gazed at that small green meadow lying distinct below the rock wall of the Cascades. That meadow surrounded by juniper, by rocks that glinted in the afternoon sun—an island of peace in the chaos surrounding him.

Pushing through a final tangle of vines, he emerged from the forest into the meadow. The grass was shiny with dew and gleamed in the moonlight.

"We're here, Elbridge," Lewis whispered. "We're here where the birds will come."

Elbridge continued his ragged breathing; he lay limp and motionless in his friend's arms. Lewis swept the meadow with his eye; a large boulder thrust up in the middle of the knoll. He dropped his canvas duffel bag from his shoulder, then knelt and sat down with his back against the east side of the rock. He positioned Elbridge on his lap, the man's head resting against his shoulder, and draped the blanket over him. Lewis tilted his head and let it rest on the cold surface of the stone; his breath came slower now, and he looked into the sky. The moon had climbed high above the mountain range but still shone on the jagged peaks. The brighter stars peeked through the moonlight.

It was not yet midnight; dawn was hours away. Lewis flexed his shoulders against the cold. Elbridge moved and coughed once. Lewis talked to him, trying to calm him and prevent another coughing spasm.

"We're out by the cornfield, Elbridge. The man just cut the corn yesterday. It's opening day of dove season, and in a little while the birds are gonna start flocking in here. They'll be thicker than flies. You hear me?"

Elbridge moved again, as if Lewis's words about doves had cut through the cloud of drugs that engulfed him.

"You just hang in there, buddy," Lewis said. "I'm gonna show you some doves."

He reared his head and focused on one of the brighter stars. "Me and you been at each other for too long. I still ain't sure who you really are, but I'm beginning to know me now. I wish you'd let this fellow hang on till the morning. I wish you'd bring some doves in here. I wish you'd let this fellow go out of here knowing what he came looking for."

Lewis stared into infinity. He took a long, deep breath.

The stars were as distinct and cold as ever, but now he saw them not as just singular points of light: they were part of something beyond description, a universe and a world and a life and a history too vast even to begin to understand.

Spark

Lewis

ALL OF LIFE is one big, slow wheel that takes us in circles.
That's what Elbridge was babbling about tonight in the
hospital when he was delirious. At first I thought it was
just more crazy talk; most of what I've heard him say
over the past few weeks seemed like crazy talk, but I'm
not so sure now. That big moon is round like a ball, and
it goes in a big circle across the sky like it was on a string.
I know the sun will come up in the morning, and it will
come up the next morning too, even if I'm not awake or
alive to see it. The air is cold right now, and the snow
is not far off, but the snow will melt in the spring and
the flowers will bloom, and the seasons will come around
and around in one big, slow circle that has been millions
and will be millions more. I can see the Big Dipper
cocked up at an angle, ready to spill water. Next month
she'll be sitting flat. She hangs on her handle like she is
pinned to the sky. I feel I've come in a circle too, back
to where I have nothing in me now, dry as this rock I'm
leaning against, brittle and cold, with nothing left except
the possibility of what can be. My mind is as open as a
baby's.

Elbridge asked me the other day, when he was co-
herent, to think about what I had felt over the past year.

At the time, I took it as more of his crazy talk, but sitting here now with only the clear sky above me, I'm starting to realize what he meant. If nothing else, since the world exploded around me, I've felt. God damn, I've felt. I've felt pain and heartache and loneliness, I've felt my own tears, and maybe for the first time in a long while, I've started to feel hope. If feelings were money, I'd be a rich man.

They say fire creates life. That sounds ironic, considering that fire in one form or another took from me and Elbridge everything we had. But this here little meadow probably was created from fire—lightning struck a tree and burned out this couple of acres, and grass and flowers grew up out of the ashes. I used to read how the universe was created from an explosion, how the volcanoes erupting built up the land, how the fish eventually crawled upon it. Out in Yellowstone, after the big forest fires sweep through and burn all the trees, plants and grass and saplings start growing soon as the ground cools, in places where there once had been just deep, gloomy shade. The whole cycle of forest starting over.

I was never one to ask a lot of questions. I always took my orders and followed them the best I could. I didn't ask for much quarter and I didn't give much. People are always saying that life doesn't have to be fair, and it's not. Not even close. If I don't freeze sitting here tonight, I'll feel the sun warm my face tomorrow, but this guy here in my lap ain't going to feel it.

Yeah, I've felt some things, Elbridge. Most of them I'd soon as done without, but I've felt. I hope that somehow between now and the morning, some of it begins to make sense.

I do know one thing, and I realize this as well as I

know this ground is hard and this air is cold. I ain't the man I was. I don't even know if I'm still a man at all, or something between man and snake and freak. Fire will make a steel rod drip like water. Is it still a steel rod?

I was once tough as steel. People said I was, anyway. I didn't start out so tough, but growing up made me that way. I remember a child. It seems now that he lived a million years ago.

The chug, chug of the tractor could be heard from the barn, growing louder by the second, like approaching feet. Lewis stuffed the last of his cheese nabs into his mouth and bubbled his Pepsi, the sweet soda lukewarm in the hot August air. The leaves on the tobacco stalks had been pulled halfway to the top and offered little shade from the glaring sun. Lewis stuck his empty bottle neck-first in the ground, then scooped a palmful of dirt and rubbed it over his hands to take some of the stickiness from the tobacco gum that coated his fingers.

He stared at the other croppers, who sat under their own stalks hurrying through their late-morning snack, and arched his shoulders and stretched, trying to loosen the knot of muscles in his back that ached from bending over. He listened to the tractor as it languished in the half-minute before it would be time to stand again and bend and snatch tobacco leaves. The croppers had started in the field when the sun was only a white, muted disk in the dawn fog, and they would fill the last trailer when the sun was swollen and red and hung just above the treeline to the west.

"Y'all better get on up," said Cappy, an old black man

who wore a red bandana around his head. "The monkey liable to crawl on your back while you sitting down."

Lewis knew the monkey. The monkey was the croppers' name for heat exhaustion, and he'd had his virgin bout with it the year before, when he had first come to the field to work. He knew now to always wear a hat and to drink water between rows and not to race to the end of the field. He stood up slowly and watched the tractor come down the drag row. Lewis glanced around at the five other croppers in his group, all of them older than he, and all of them, unlike him, black. Sweat had dried on their faces, and their forearms and hands were caked with tobacco gum. Lewis squinted at the sun and reckoned the time to be about eleven: still an hour or so of work before they would ride in on the load, then pile into the bed of the pickup truck with the barn help and go to Johnson's store to buy lunch, which they ate in the shade of the big oak trees out front.

The tractor driver jammed on the brakes when he was beside the croppers, and slid to a stop. "Dive in, lads," a white boy in his early teens smirked. "Damn 'baccor is burning up in the fields."

The boy's face split with a mean smile. This was Carter's son, a cocky fellow a couple of years older than Lewis who got to sit atop the tractor under a tarp all day and not bend his back in the field. Lewis swore under his breath.

Lewis had worked for Carter since he was eight years old, first with the women and other children at the barn, where the leaves were looped to tobacco sticks, then with the men in the field, where he earned twice the money but did three times more labor. But he was glad for the work. The dollars helped him and his father through the hard times, when his father got sick on whiskey.

Now in the field, Lewis stooped and began to crop. North Carolina bright-leaf tobacco—step forward, back bent; curl your fingers around the stalk and snap off the bottom three or four ripe leaves; swing them to your other side and tuck them under your armpit; step forward and pull the leaves from the next stalk, and the next, and the next, until your armload is as full as you can hold. Then step across the row to the tractor-trailer and lay the leaves down, stems to the outside, hurry back to your row, and start over again. Lewis had learned the work, was able to keep up with the tractor and the other croppers. He fixed his mind on the money he would have earned at the end of the day. Four more trailers had been filled when Carter blew his truck horn signaling the croppers to come in for lunch.

The chance to stand tall on the rear of the trailer for the ride back to the barn was almost worth the sweat and backache of the morning. The women and children would look up from where they were handing and looping tobacco as the tractor roared in, and the croppers would swagger from the trailer into the shade of the trees, playing to the hilt that they were above barn help. Lewis remembered too well the years he had watched the croppers come in from the field and longed to be one of them. For these few minutes now it didn't matter to him that he had a full afternoon of work left, or that after the last leaf of tobacco was pulled, he and the rest of the croppers would have to hang the heavy sticks of tobacco in the barn, to be cured by the heat of fire. For these moments, even with the tar and dirt that covered his hands, wearing sweat-moistened clothes and barely twelve years old, he was a man.

Johnson's Food & Seed sat at a crossroads under two giant oaks. An assortment of canned and dry goods packed the wall and aisle shelves, and a cooler chest was filled with cold sodas, hoop cheese, and fat loaves of bologna and ham that could be sliced to order. Lewis took his time selecting lunch. Supper at home was usually a TV dinner or hot dogs between slices of folded white bread; he splurged on lunch, knowing his tab would be taken out of his pay and he'd never even miss it. He decided on a can of spaghetti and meatballs, saltines, a honey bun, and two cold Pepsis.

"Hungry, ain't you, son?" Mr. Johnson said as he rang up the order. "The way you sprouting, you need to eat." He scribbled the charge for Lewis's food in a notebook.

Lewis waited in line to wash his hands under the cold-water spigot with a bar of rough Lava soap. After scraping off most of the tobacco tar, he slung his hands back and forth to dry them. His stomach growled at the prospect of food, and he found an empty spot on a root under one of the oaks. The laborers were in little groups, the older women chattering, the younger people stuffing their mouths and listening. Lewis lifted the first Pepsi and drained half of it. His spaghetti was glutinous and cold and delicious; he used a plastic spoon to cut the meatballs into slices, then ate them on top of crackers. After finishing the first Pepsi, he consumed his honey bun, slowly chewing off small bites and rolling the sweet dough across his tongue before swallowing.

Nature was calling and Lewis needed to get in line outside the small bathroom at the rear of the store. He carefully propped his soda against the tree root. He returned ten minutes later, prepared to close his eyes and rest until Carter came tooting his horn, rushing everyone back to the field.

Lewis reached for his second Pepsi, lifted it and began

drinking, then gagged and spit a mouthful of soda on the ground. In the puddle of liquid lay a fat green tobacco worm. Lewis's stomach heaved at the sight. He heard laughter and jerked his eyes up to see two black teenagers watching him, big grins on their faces. They looked away quickly.

The tobacco worm was still alive and was trying to crawl out of the puddle of soda. Lewis stood and stomped the worm under his heel. When he glanced up he saw the black guys grinning again. He walked over to where they sat on a discarded tractor tire.

"Who put that worm in my drink?" he asked the one named Dexter.

"What you talking 'bout?" Dexter said.

"Did you put that tobacco worm in my drink?"

Dexter nodded toward his friend. "What this fool talking 'bout. Worms in his soda."

"You put it in there, didn't you?" Lewis asked. He didn't know the two boys very well. They had started just that week, hired by Carter from out of project housing on the edge of town.

"You better get your honky ass away from here. I don't play with no worms."

"You owe me a new soda."

Dexter, who stood several inches taller than Lewis, jabbed his finger into the younger boy's chest. "Listen, you better haul your white-trash ass back on over there. I don't owe you shit."

"You owe me a Pepsi."

Dexter shoved him backward. Lewis lost his footing and went down hard on his rump. He leaped up, his hands balled into fists. A knot of fear twisted in his belly.

"Come on over here with them fists," Dexter said. "I

kick your white-trash ass. Standing there, your pants up above your ankles. I seen where you live this morning.''

Lewis breathed fast, and blinked to fight the threat of tears.

Cappy rose from where he was sitting on an upturned bucket. "You boys best save yo' energy. There's a whole half a field and a barn to hang 'fore you get home."

"White boy fixing to get his ass kicked, old man," Dexter said.

"There ain't no color out here, boy, 'cept green," Cappy replied. "Green 'baccor and green money. Far as trash is concerned, I don't believe you come from the Taj Mahal."

Dexter glared at Cappy, mumbled under his breath, and turned away. Lewis walked back to the tree. He flung his soda bottle into some bushes and sat down. *White trash.* He'd heard that more times in his life than he liked to remember. He tugged at the short cuffs on his trousers, which he'd gotten a few months earlier in a large sack of clothes from the social worker. Either his clothes were shrinking or he was growing like a weed, as Mr. Johnson had said. Lewis shut his eyes and settled against the tree, trying to let go of his anger. He'd had his eyes closed for only a few minutes when he heard the grind of tires on gravel and the blare of Carter's truck horn.

Row after row of tobacco plants. Walking bent over, snatching the leaves and cramming them under his arm until he had a full load. The sun shone silver and hot against a hazy sky. In the late afternoon, clouds began to bunch on the horizon and the growl of distant thunder could be heard. Despite the heat, Lewis hoped a storm wouldn't roll in and stop work. He had his mind on a new bicycle with hand brakes he had seen at the

Western Auto store. The clouds slid above the treeline
to the north, the thunder growing long and rumbly like
a far-off train. Lewis was still angry about the worm in
his Pepsi, and embarrassed at having been shoved down
in front of so many people. His only consolation was that
the two new croppers weren't used to the heat and had
to keep stopping to mop their foreheads with sweat-
soaked rags while bringing up the rear. He hoped the
monkey jumped on both of them.

Five o'clock had just passed, and the last trailer was
filled. The croppers climbed onto the trailer and the
fenders of the tractor. Carter's son rammed the tractor
into gear and roared toward the barn, the laborers hanging
on as if they were riding a wild chariot. This time when
they reached the barn, there were no minutes in which
to loiter. A few hundred sticks of green tobacco were
piled near the barn door, ready to be hung on the pole
rafters. Hanging was the worst part of working the crop.

The tobacco barn was a square log building three stories tall. The various levels of rafters that ran its length
and divided it into what were called rooms were just far
enough apart that the four-foot-long sticks of tobacco
could be hung on them. The croppers, two to a team,
stood on the rafters, one higher than another, and the
cropper below passed the tobacco sticks to the cropper
above, who hung them on the rafters above and below
him. Standing spread-legged and lifting forty-pound
sticks of green leaf took balance and strength; the barn
was dusty and even hotter than the field. The croppers
took turns handing up and hanging.

Two rooms were left to hang when Carter pointed at
Lewis and Dexter and told them to go up.

"I got the bottom," Dexter demanded.

"Don't matter to me," Lewis answered. He quickly

climbed the rafters. The top was better, he thought, even though you were high off the ground. At least on top you didn't have to lift the sticks over your head. The two boys proceeded in silence, hanging the sticks about a foot apart on the rafters, so the heat could circulate when the burners were on. The air up high in the barn was stifling; the leaves were still damp from the morning dew, and sand and drops of water fell in a steady rain. As Lewis and Dexter worked their way, their sweat dripped and mixed with the shower from the leaves.

Halfway down the room, Lewis stopped at the sight of a rat snake coiled on a rafter below him, a yard or two away. The snake, as thick as his wrist and about five feet long, was motionless except for its tongue, which flicked out occasionally; otherwise the snake was frozen in place, as if trying to hide. After the initial scare at seeing the snake, Lewis took a deep breath to slow his heart. He knew rat snakes weren't poisonous; the barn hadn't been fired yet this summer, and the snake had probably been living there since the spring, catching and eating mice and birds.

He placed his tobacco sticks carefully, moving away from the snake so as not to disturb it. With a mix of amusement and dread, he saw that Dexter would soon be even with the snake, his head level with the rafter the serpent lay on. Lewis clenched his jaw.

Dexter had taken a step backward and was fitting a stick onto the rafters when he saw the snake. He gasped, moved to the side, and slipped and fell, dragging down two sticks of tobacco with him. He hit the ground with a thud, then jumped up and raced to the door in one fluid motion.

"God damn almighty," Dexter hollered. "Muthafuckin' snake big as my leg."

"What the hell is going on?" Carter stepped into the barn and frowned at the broken leaves on the floor.

"Muthafuckin' snake up there."

"That snake ain't gonna hurt you," Lewis called from above. He gritted his teeth to keep from laughing.

"Muthafucka, you saw that damn snake," Dexter shouted. "You come your white ass down here, and I'll break your head."

Lewis bent and reached slowly until his hand was behind the snake's head, and then grabbed the creature by the neck. The snake writhed and wrapped around his arm, then emptied its bowels, emitting a strong musk smell. Lewis climbed down, holding the snake.

The second his feet hit the ground, the barn cleared except for Carter. "Throw that thing out in the weeds, son," Carter said. "We got to finish this barn." He walked out of the gloom of the barn into daylight. Lewis stood still and listened to the voices around him.

"I ain't doing this shit no mo'," he heard Dexter say. "You can pay me off right now. I ain't going back in no barn or no field."

Lewis chuckled. He envisioned a cold Pepsi, the bottle beaded with dew, minus any tobacco worms.

Elbridge

I'VE SLIPPED OUT OF MYSELF. I thought at first I was having another dream, but I don't think so now. This is real. It's like I'm half in a sleeping bag and half out of it, my body warm and my heart still beating slow and regular, but my mind outside. I can see the moon in the sky over those mountains and several bright stars that shine through the glow. I'm looking down from a couple of feet above Lewis; he's sitting against a big rock and holding someone in his lap all bundled up in a blanket. It's me. I can breathe again, and I don't hurt. I can't feel the cold. My mind is like clear water, running full and strong. If it's really a dream, it's the best one I've had since the fire.

"Lewis, can you hear me? It's me, Elbridge." He doesn't move, so I guess I'm not speaking in words. He's just sitting there with his shoulders hunched against the cold; I can see his mouth quivering a little. I wish I could wrap all around him and hug up to him like he's doing to me, and let him feel some of this peace. I can't see my body under that blanket, the way he's got it folded all around me, but I can see the blanket rise and fall real slow with my breath.

More and more stars are coming out, like the sky is being lowered closer and closer to me. I have this urge to take one final breath and slide on out of what ties me to that blanket, but something is holding me like I'm intertwined with the threads of wool. I have a feeling I don't know how to describe. The best way I can put it into words is to say I'm standing right outside a door, and I know right behind that door is something I've been wanting since I was born. I guess Lewis would say it is more of my crazy talk, but I know different. Did you ever wake up from a dream, and you knew it was a good one, but the memory was hidden deep inside your brain and wouldn't come forward? I wish that door would go ahead and open.

This darkness and moonlight takes all the color out of

the world. Everything is black-and-white. Lewis has his
eye closed, and the muscles in his jaw seem smooth and
relaxed. I can't see the pink scars on his face. He looks
the most peaceful he's looked since that day I first saw
him face to face. That day seems like both years and
only seconds behind me, as if time had stopped. I can
hear Lewis's breath coming long and slow from his lips,
like he's dozing. I wish I could see myself under that
blanket and know if the color in me has been erased too.
Just black-and-white is how I'd like it, one no better than
the other. I wish I could reach out now and open that
door, but my hands are still under that blanket; what
hangs here in the moonlight is only a mind and a memory.

I'm Elbridge Snipes. I never knew who my daddy was.
They say my mama run off when I was still nursing. My
grandpa raised me in a small house in a mountain hollow
in eastern Kentucky. He worked in the coal mines until
his lungs got bad, and then he fed me and him on the
government check he got each month, helped along by
the chickens we raised and the garden we grew behind
the house and the game birds he liked to hunt.

I remember being six years old and digging potatoes.
It must have been early June, the weather was warm,
the tomato bushes had little green fruit and the squash
was in full bloom. Me and Grandpa had been eating
spinach and green onions and radishes already for several
weeks. He would put all three vegetables together in a
fry pan and wilt them down with bacon grease. But the
potatoes were the first real food to come off. The old
man walked in front of me with a hooked garden fork,
pulling each plant out by the roots, then raking the soil

from about six inches deep. Those potatoes rolled up like jewels, red as a sunset. I dug down in the dirt and pulled out the potatoes and laid them in a reed basket. In a quart mason jar, I dropped every grub and earthworm I turned up, thinking about the fishing we'd do that afternoon in the branch that flowed in the ravine below the house. The brim were still on the bed, and they'd snag a worm as soon as it hit the water.

"The fruit of the lan'," I remember my grandpa saying. "We're eating off the table of the fruit of the lan'." He was not a churchgoing man, but he sometimes talked like a preacher.

"Boy," he would tell me, "people ain't much different from seeds. First you cull out the bad ones, the puny ones. Good soil under your feet, water and sun. Keep the weeds pulled out before they get too deeply rooted. A seed or a boy, they both will sprout and grow tall toward the sun." For years while I was growing up, I thought I was one of the bad seed.

I never knew there was anything different about me until I entered first grade. The school that taught my community contained all twelve grades and still had only about a hundred students. I remember riding home on the school bus early in the school year and having this older kid come and sit down in the seat in front of me.

"Who's your daddy?" he asked.

I hung my head a little. "My grandpa is my daddy."

"He ain't your real daddy. You a bastard, ain't you?"

I didn't know what a bastard was. "I'm a Snipes."

The boy laughed. "Yeah, you a bastard all right. A half-breed nigger bastard with blue eyes."

I asked my grandpa that night over supper what a nigger bastard was. He didn't look up from his plate for several moments, and when he did, his eyes were shiny. "Them words ain't nothing, son. They don't mean a thing. You come from good stock. My mama was a full-bloodied Pawnee Indian."

"Why'd my mama leave?"

He carefully forked several butter beans. "I don't know. I guess she was too young and restless. That's for the Lord to know. Man, he ain't supposed to know some things."

I studied my face in the mirror that night. I couldn't turn away from the fact that I didn't look much like my grandpa, even less like the other kids in my class. I had full lips and a nose that lay flat and wide. My eyes were a clear, light blue that looked even brighter against my brown skin. My hair was what seemed most different. It grew thick and curly as sheep's wool and was as orange as the carrots we dug from the garden. I still didn't know what a bastard was, but I sure didn't look like any of the Indians I'd seen in the movies on our old black-and-white television. I didn't look much like the natives on Tarzan movies neither, running around half naked.

Over the next few years I found out what a half-breed nigger was. He was someone who didn't get valentines in his pouch, except for one from the teacher and one from Holly Ridgeway, the preacher's daughter. A half-breed nigger didn't get picked until last to play ball, and he wasn't ever invited home by someone to spend the night. It didn't matter that my clothes were no shabbier than the other boys' or that I could spell and read just as good as anyone—that orange kinky hair of mine kept people at a distance like my head was on fire. I found out another thing too: A half-breed nigger had to learn to use his fists.

"Yo' mama fucked a nigger, then ran off with him," Willie Bedsoe taunted me at recess. "You look like one of them mongrel dogs they gas to death down at the pound."

A crowd of boys and girls stood in a circle around us, most of the boys smiling, the girls watching with their faces bunched up. I was always little for my age, but when I hit Willie that first time, my fist seemed to draw back from years and miles. I caught him right in the nose, and the blood spurted. He hollered and doubled over, and the next thing I knew, the teacher was dragging me to the office, where the principal got out his big wooden paddle with holes drilled in it and proceeded to give me five hard licks.

Willie never called me a nigger again or talked about my mama, and if anyone else did, I swung hard and took whatever came to me, be it a thrashing by an older, tougher kid, or another whipping with the principal's paddle.

One day when I was twelve, I came home from school to find something wrapped in a newspaper lying on the kitchen table, with my name on it. I ripped off the paper and found a brand-new Remington twelve-gauge pump-action shotgun. I stared at it for several seconds, like I was holding something alive and hot, then ran outside to find Grandpa cutting okra in our late-summer garden. I held the gun up and looked at him. Except for clothes and a few cheap toys for Christmas, his government check had always gone for our needs.

"You know a gun can kill you, don't you?" he said.

I nodded.

"It can kill you like a snake if you let it. Don't ever forget that. But it can feed you too. And it can free you from the world. Maybe for just an hour or so, but it can free you."

I wasn't sure what this freedom he spoke of was. He slowly folded the knife he had been using, then took the gun from my hands and showed me how to load it, where the safety was, and how to sight down the barrel. That night he gave me a box of shells. I spent the next couple of afternoons shooting pine cones out of trees. The following Saturday morning, before the sun had risen, we stood at the edge of a field where the corn had been cut recently. I gripped my new shotgun. My grandpa held his old double-barrel with the twin brass triggers.

"Boy, you got to think of this gun as a part of your eye. Where your eye looks, that barrel is pointing. The bird'll come in here faster than you can blink, but you lock on it with your eye and lead it, and you knock it down."

The morning was cool and foggy, and I felt a lump in my stomach even cooler than the air. The sun was still a red glow in the east.

"You can't worry about it. There ain't no time to talk or reason. You got to just be part of something bigger than you. Throw that gun up and lock on your eye, and when it's time to shoot, you'll know it."

The sun had barely crested the treetops when a flight of doves came in low over the field, thinking of settling to eat the scattered kernels of corn. The birds seen us and turned broadside, winging up like someone had thrown them. I raised the gun and tried to train on one of the birds, but my finger was too tight on the trigger and the shell exploded with a bump into my shoulder. I forgot to jack in another shell and pulled the trigger again, only to silence. My grandpa squeezed off both his triggers and two doves fell.

"Don't think," Grandpa said. "Just react. You got to let yourself become part of something that's bigger than you."

Several more flights of birds passed over. I shot five or six times but didn't even get any feathers. The old man knocked a bird down each time. I was feeling bad, when a single bird passed over the treeline and came across the field at an angle to us.

"Take him," the old man said.

I threw that gun barrel up and sighted in on the bird. I saw him there in the bright bead at the end of the sights, the sky blue behind him; I led him the span of my hand and squeezed the trigger. Feathers exploded around him, and he fell, wings trailing in a V, toward the ground. I raced out in the field to get him. The dove lay there stone dead in the stubble of cut corn, the sunlight reflecting in shades of blue on his wing feathers. It was the first thing I'd killed in my life except for bugs and worms and snakes. But I didn't feel bad about it. I knew I'd eat that dove, and even more, I knew I'd found something I could do that I didn't have to ask help with or be judged on by someone who didn't like my lips or hair. It was just me and my eye and, as the old man had said, letting myself become a part of something that could free me. I stuffed the dove in my coat pocket. Before we left the field at noontime, I'd gotten three more doves, and for once in my life, I felt proud.

I quit school the day I turned sixteen. The fistfights and failed classes had killed my desire to learn. I could write and read and didn't feel the need for much else.

All I had ever seen the men around home do was go down into coal mines; algebra wouldn't make that easier. I applied for my union card and waited. I hunted turkeys on the ridge above the house, learned how to sit silently for an hour and call a big tom in where he'd come all puffed up and strutting, thinking I was a lady friend, and then I'd lay him out with a clean shot to the head. I spent a lot of hours in the woods.

Me and Grandpa were breaking up the ground for the spring garden late one March, when suddenly the old man stopped still in his tracks and looked at me with his eyes wide like he saw something big. He straightened his back and set his jaw hard, then reached into his back pocket and took out his handkerchief. I watched him without saying anything as he kneeled and placed his handkerchief on the ground, then leaned over and rested his forehead against it. He twitched once and moaned, and I saw piss spread dark against his trouser legs.

"Grandpa?" I said.

He twitched again, then rolled to his side, and when I put my hand on his shoulder, I knew he was dead.

The day after he was buried, I packed what few things I had. The house and land were rented, and I knew if I ever went down into that coal mine, I'd never leave it, and till I died I'd be fighting the coal and every man who laughed at me. I hitched a satchel over my back, gripped the sling on my shotgun, and began climbing that first ridge above the house.

Lewis

THERE'S A BREEZE in the air tonight, and sometimes it sounds like voices to me. Like someone whispering real low. Elbridge moved a couple of times and I thought he might be waking up, but I rocked him a little and he got still again. I hope he sleeps and doesn't have another of his coughing fits. I don't know if he would last another one without an oxygen mask. I hope he'll lie here and sleep and not wake up till the morning, and if there are such things as miracles, I hope some doves will fly in here so he can see them.

This is going to be one long, cold night. Twice already I've reached over and touched that fifth of vodka in my sack and thought about how good it would taste burning a path down my throat. But both times I took my hand off it. I ain't going to let it control me any longer. At least not until the morning comes, and whatever is going to happen does.

I wish that wind *would* speak to me. I wish it would tell me why I'm sitting here holding this fellow on a mountainside, both of us thousands of miles from home. I wish it would explain to me all the shit that's happened over the past year. I don't know if there is any answer for it now, but I feel something coming from that moon-glow and from those stars. Speak to me, wind.

*

Lewis asked Carter to let him out of the truck when they were a half-mile from the house. The sun was behind the trees, and the mourning doves were cooing from their roosts in the pine-tops, while frogs and crickets had begun to chirp in the water of the roadside ditch. Lewis walked slowly, enjoying the chorus of nature and the tufts of red clouds in the west. He patted his shirt pocket and felt the wad of folded money: sixty-six dollars clear, eating expenses deducted—sweat money if ever there was, and he had earned every penny. He would stuff the bills in the sock he kept under his mattress, along with the other money he'd saved, and when school started three weeks later he would wear new blue jeans and sneakers, instead of the hand-me-downs the other kids laughed at.

Lewis could see a single light burning in the window at home. The house was old and unpainted, a squat four-room dwelling that sagged like it was tired. His father's pickup was in the driveway. Joe, their black-and-tan coon hound, scented when Lewis was fifty yards from the house, and trotted from the front porch to the road, where he barked happily and wagged his tail. The hound sniffed Lewis's legs while the boy scraped his boots against the bottom step. From inside the house, Lewis could hear Tammy Wynette on the radio. He opened the door and saw his father sitting at the table, his head propped on one arm, staring into space. On the table was a fifth of Canadian Mist beside a bottle of Mountain Dew and a Dixie cup. His father turned at the squeak of the door.

"Hey, Lewie, I was wondering when you'd git here."

Lewis glanced at the whiskey bottle to see how empty it was. Only a couple of fingers had been drunk. "We had to fill two barns today. Carter's going to fire them tonight."

His father was a large man with thick black hair. A prominent chin and a hawk-bill nose made him look mean when he wasn't smiling. He was smiling tonight: whiskey always made him smile—at least in the beginning. He pulled out a chair. "Sit down here and rest and tell me about it. Son, I spent my time in them fields. It'll make a man of you, it'll do that for sure."

Lewis stood behind the chair. "Why don't I fix us some supper," he said. "I think there's hamburger in the fridge."

"Aw, hell, sit down and rest. It's Friday night. Payday. In a while we'll ride up to Western Sizzlin and get us a steak. Get you some ice in a glass and I'll pour you some soda. I know you're thirsty." He reached for the whiskey and very carefully poured a double shot in his cup, then added Mountain Dew. "How 'bout getting me some more ice while you're up."

Lewis went to the refrigerator and looked inside: a carton of milk and a few eggs, some chicken franks and a package of hamburger. The bottom shelf was filled with six-packs of Budweiser. He opened the freezer compartment and took out an ice-cube tray.

Lewis never understood what brought on his father's whiskey drunks. He did all right when he stuck to beer— a case a day, the first can opened at breakfast, the last before going to bed. He worked five days a week as a plumber, and no one would know he was drinking except for the smell on his breath. But every few months he'd start in on the whiskey, and before he stopped, he'd be talking out of his head, vomiting blood, and the social worker would come and take Lewis to stay with Mrs. Bullard.

Lewis dropped two ice cubes into his father's cup.

"You go get cleaned up some. Me and you gonna get us a steak. One of them big rib-eyes."

Lewis went into the bathroom. He stripped off his dirty clothes and turned on the shower, then waited until the water was steaming hot. He scrubbed himself with a washrag until the tobacco tar came off, leaving his skin bright pink. In the bedroom he shared with his father, he hunted through the dresser until he found a pair of jeans, faded but clean, and a T-shirt. In the corner of the drawer lay the old tattered Bible he had discovered stuffed in the back of the closet, and he opened it.

A yellowed photograph of his mother and father lay beneath the cover. Lewis lifted the picture and studied it. His father was young and handsome in his Marine uniform, his mother raven-haired and smiling in a lacy dress and a flowered bonnet. They stood on the steps of a church, holding hands. Written inside the cover of the Bible were the words: *Bill and Debra Calhoon, married June 10, 1953. Till death do us part.*

Lewis looked once more at his mother's face, then returned the photograph to the Bible and closed it. She had died from an infection, two days after his birth.

Lewis pulled on his jeans. They were a little tight, so he did a few knee bends to stretch the fabric. He heard his father's footsteps in the kitchen, then the click of the television in the living room, and Walter Cronkite's voice. Lewis put on a pair of clean socks, then his boots, still grimy with dirt from the tobacco field.

His father was pouring himself another drink when Lewis walked into the living room.

"I'm ready, Dad," Lewis said.

"Yeah, wait just a minute. We'll go in just a minute." He lifted his cup and drank. The television was showing combat footage from Vietnam. His father stared intently at the screen and poured himself another drink without looking. "Goddamn Vietnam," he said. "You could take any bum off the street and he'd do better than Johnson is doing. Don't nobody want to take charge. Everybody from the president to the generals on down are scared they'll do something wrong."

"We ought to go to the steakhouse before it gets too crowded, Dad." Lewis studied the whiskey bottle.

"Yeah, just a minute. We'll go." His father took another long swallow. "Used to be, there was a thing called the chain of command. You took your orders and passed them on." He gazed above the television, his eyes glassy. "We were surrounded once. Goddamn Koreans so close you could hit one with a rock. The lieutenant took a bullet and went down. The gunny sergeant—what was his name?—Vasquez, Gunny Vasquez, yeah, he took over. Grenade knocked him out, and the buck sergeant was top. He went down. All of a sudden, I was the senior man, and I was just a corporal. It was up to me or we'd all die. Do you think I tried to pass the buck? Do you?"

"No, Dad."

"Hell no, I didn't. I called the platoon into a wedge, and I took the point, and we went over that hill and lived." He emptied his cup. "Boy, you got to take charge of your life. Stay in control. They'll shoot you dead. They'll shoot you goddamn dead."

"I know, Dad. We ought to go before it gets too late."

"Yeah, yeah, there ain't no rush. Just relax a minute, the way you been working all week. We gonna go. Get us a big steak."

Thirty minutes later, his father was talking to himself, babbling on with words that didn't make sense. The whiskey bottle was three-quarters empty, and Lewis wondered whether there was another one stashed in the truck. When his father's head started to bob, Lewis got up from the couch and went into the kitchen. He took a frying pan and put it on the stove to heat, then mashed out two large hamburger patties and dropped them in hot grease.

Led by the organ's mournful music, the choir began the first verse of "Just As I Am." The preacher stood before the congregation, his face uplifted, his eyes narrowed and intense as if he saw something beyond the church ceiling. Lewis was in the front row, beside Mrs. Bullard, where he was always made to sit. Her own three sons were allowed to go in the balcony, where most of the other young people congregated. Lewis fixed his eyes on the picture in the baptistery, of the river Jordan flowing through a green valley; a lion lay beside a lamb in the grass; people with wings strolled hand in hand.

"Won't you come now to the Lord," the preacher said above the drone of voices. "Won't you come and be saved."

Lewis gripped the edges of the bench so hard that his knuckles turned white. He stared again into the picture and tried to imagine eternity. To live forever and ever was to him a terrifying thought—especially if it meant being in a place like the one in the painting, surrounded by angels who sang like the people in church.

He never had been fond of church. His father never went, for, as he said, "Me and God have an agreement. I won't hold Him responsible for all the crap that happens in the world as long as He leaves me alone."

The only times Lewis did attend the River Wood Baptist Church were when he had to stay with Mrs. Bullard. He had given vacation Bible school a try once, because word was you got Kool-Aid and cookies at midmorning. But after just two days, he realized the snack wasn't worth having to read Bible verses aloud and sit in a chair all morning.

Mrs. Bullard made sure he went to church every Sunday, bright and early, when she had him in her care. She would give him one of her oldest son's suits to wear— never the right size—and take him to the Sunday-school class she taught, and then to the front row of the chapel for services. As sure as clockwork, every Sunday during the first hymn, she would stand and walk toward the preacher. She would clasp his hands in hers and whisper something in his ear, the preacher would nod and smile, and she would return to her seat, her face as serene as that of the angels in the painting.

"Jesus loves you," the preacher was saying. "His love is like a mighty river ready to wash all your sins away."

Lewis didn't have much faith in the word "love." He had never once heard his father say it; he couldn't remember ever saying the word to his father. The only person who said it was Mrs. Bullard.

"Oh, we're glad to have him," she had told the social worker who brought Lewis over. "We love him like one of our own."

"Well, I don't know for sure how long he'll be here this time," the social worker had said. "Mr. Calhoon was in pretty bad shape when I saw him."

Mrs. Bullard had clasped her hand on Lewis's shoulder. "Oh, it doesn't matter if he stays a month. We love him to death."

"Just walk forward," the preacher continued. "People

will let you go by. Jesus wants you to confess your sins, and He'll wash you of them. With His blood and tears He'll make you pure."

Blood and tears weren't supposed to go together. That was a rule Lewis's father had taught him. He had been only eight and was helping his father drag pipes into a house under construction. A six-penny nail had rammed through the sole of his sneaker and into the soft flesh between two toes. Lewis's eyes welled up as his father took a pair of pliers from his tool belt.

"Don't cry. Stop those tears right now," his father had said. "Just get mad. Crying makes you weak."

Lewis had gritted his teeth and wiped his face. He gritted them again when the nurse stuck him with the needle for a tetanus shot. On his father's next payday, Lewis came home from school to find a new pair of boots on his bed, with inch-thick leather soles and a stainless mesh insole.

What did Mrs. Bullard tell the preacher every Sunday? Lewis wondered. Did she tell him she was sorry for making her foster son sit in a dark closet because he dropped and broke a dinner plate, for repeating to him he was white trash and his father was a drunk, for always looking the other way when her boys ganged up and popped him with their knuckles on the top of his head? Lying was supposed to be a sin, and hadn't he heard her say she loved him like one of her own?

Squeezing the bench, Lewis fought off the thoughts of his sins. He'd told a few lies and cheated a couple of times on tests at school. He'd learned how to cuss in the tobacco fields, had stared openmouthed at the pictures in a *Playboy* that one of the older croppers had brought and shown at lunch. He remembered his sins most on the summer nights when big storms rolled in and the wind howled and thunder burst in the same instant that lightning sizzled down the tall oak trees. He'd crawl under the cover beside his father, and though the man's breath smelled of beer, Lewis felt safer there against his warm chest. Before the light of morning, he'd slip from beneath the sheet and return to his own bed. But regardless of his sins, Lewis never walked forward at church. It didn't seem right that Mrs. Bullard could march up each week and return to her seat with her face as peaceful as river water, and then later that afternoon say the things that came from her mouth and do the things she did.

Lewis felt relief when the organ finally stopped and the preacher dropped his head and began praying. He hoped to be able to return home before another Sunday rolled around.

Lewis faced the front door and wondered what gift he'd find on his bed. Whenever he returned from Mrs. Bullard's, something was there—a baseball glove or a fishing rod, a model airplane or a football. His father would never talk about the time they'd been apart. He would walk in the house and shake hands, and they'd go on with life.

The coon hound thumped his tail and wiggled as Lewis walked up the steps. Rabbit fur littered the porch; the dog had had to hunt his meals in their absence. Lewis's father wasn't home yet, so he found the front door key in its place, under a brick atop the windowsill. The house smelled of Clorox, and washed dishes were stacked beside the sink in the kitchen; his father always had one of the black women who lived down the road come and clean. Lewis went to the bedroom. On top of the quilt on his bed was a long cardboard box. He ripped open the end flap and pulled out a Winchester thirty-thirty lever-action; the steel barrel was blued, the stock made of polished walnut. Holding it in both hands, Lewis tested the heft of the weapon. He worked the bolt and liked at once how the metal parts slid as smooth as silk. An air rifle had arrived two years before, but this gun was no toy: it was as big a change as the stirrings he felt in his own body—the crack in his voice, hair growing where there had been none.

His father arrived home at five-thirty. His eyes were clear again. "Hey, Lewis," he said, walking to the boy and shaking his hand. He held a package up. "I got us some steaks here."

The boy ached to hug his father, but there was always that wall between them. "Thanks for the rifle, Dad. It's the best thing I ever had."

Lewis followed his father into the kitchen, where he laid the steaks on the counter and took a beer from the refrigerator. "I started hunting when I was your age," he said. "Free meat you can't pass up." He opened the can and gulped. "But it's more than that. For me it was. I hope it's there for you too."

"What's that, Dad?"

"Up in that tree stand, waiting for the sun to come up. You feel things you don't other times. I never was a church man, but I've felt things in a tree stand I couldn't explain. You feel . . . you feel . . . Aw, hell. Go get that rifle and I'll show you how to load it."

Lewis hurried to the bedroom and back.

"Son, you got to look at a rifle as being the same thing as the defense in football. A gun will protect you. It'll keep hunger from you, and if it comes to that, it'll keep death from you. But don't ever use a gun to take something you don't need. You understand me?"

Lewis nodded. The image of the framed Bronze Star citation his father had been given after stopping the enemy from taking that hill in Korea popped into his mind.

"There ain't no pleasure in killing something. But if you're lucky, there's something else you'll find in those woods that a man can't buy with money. This rifle is just a ticket to it."

Lewis slowly nodded again. He had never heard his father talk this way.

"Tomorrow's Friday," his father continued. "After I get home, I'll put a scope on it, and we'll true up the sights. I ain't making you hunt, son, but gun season starts next week. I know a couple of good stands."

"I'd like that, Dad. I'd like it a lot."

Lewis stared into his father's eyes. The man held the gaze for only a second, then turned his back. "I'm hungry as a bear," he said. "Go put your gun up, and I'll start frying up this meat."

The first morning of deer season, Lewis's father awakened him before dawn, a cup of steaming coffee in hand. "Get dressed. We're going to the woods."

Lewis scrambled from bed and put on several layers of clothes, a lined field jacket last. On the kitchen table he found a Pop-Tart and a glass of milk. Soon he and his father were outside, walking silently across the field beside the house. The clouds above the eastern treeline were just now turning pink; the air was only a few degrees above freezing. His father shined his flashlight on their path.

A hundred yards into the forest, Lewis's father stopped at the base of a large oak. He scanned the tree trunk with the light. A crude ladder was nailed to the trunk. Lewis followed the beam of light to where it shone on a weathered platform in the fork of a branch fifteen feet above his head. A rope hung from the tree stand.

"Chamber a round and make sure it's on safety," his father said.

Lewis jacked in a round.

"Always tie your rifle barrel down. Climb up and pull the gun up to you."

Lewis hesitated, staring into the dark branches. "I need the light, don't I?"

"No. You need your eyes to get used to the dark. Climb on up."

"Ain't you coming too?"

"No. There's not room for both of us. Besides, deer hunting is something you do alone."

"But I don't know what to do, Dad."

"You just sit still and look and wait, and if you see a buck that's within range, you kill it. Just let your mind open up. If it's meant, you'll feel something you ain't felt before."

Lewis had never known such darkness and silence— he felt like the only living person on earth. Gradually the dawn brightened, until he was able to see the forest floor, thick with saplings and downed branches. Birds twittered. The cold seeped through his boots, and he wished for another pair of socks. The sun was still below the horizon, but now tree trunks were distinguishable. He swept his head from side to side to scan the spaces between trees, and moved his feet up and down and wiggled his toes, trying to quicken the blood. One heel clunked against a board. The forest exploded with sound;

the boy jerked his eyes toward the noise and saw the white tails of several deer crashing away in the undergrowth.

"Jesus," Lewis sighed. The deer had been right underneath and he had neither seen nor heard them—they were as silent as spirits. He pressed his feet against the boards and swore not to move again.

Twenty minutes passed; the sun began to blink through the boughs. Birds flittered from branch to branch, and a squirrel chattered at Lewis from a few yards away. First came the snap of a twig; he strained to listen; then another twig broke. Lewis turned cautiously toward the noise. Another snap, and the head and neck of a buck jutted from behind a tree—a young five-pointer, his nose high to the wind, his ears perked forward. He took another step and another, until his whole body was visible between two trunks. The deer swung his head from side to side, then lowered it and nibbled at the ground.

Breathe, Lewis reminded himself. He pushed off the safety and raised the rifle to his shoulder, then moved the barrel inch by inch. When the crosshairs were trained on a spot just back of the deer's shoulder, he tightened his finger on the trigger. Then he stopped.

The buck wasn't very large. The rack would be nothing to brag about. Next year he might be an eight-pointer. The realization slapped Lewis like a hand: Here he was, in total control, the decision left only to him. He had always been under someone else's direction— following Carter's orders, complying with the social worker when his father got whiskey sick, bossed around by Mrs. Bullard and her sons. At school, he obeyed teachers' commands without question, and at home his father's, never asking why he did the things that forced him to leave. But on this bright dawn, in the cold boughs of this tree, the decision to shoot was totally up to him. A life in his own hands. Lewis lowered the rifle. "Bang," he shouted. "You're dead."

The buck flinched, then wheeled and bounded deep into the woods. Two weeks later, Lewis killed his first deer, an eight-point buck, with a clean shot through the heart.

Elbridge

I SPENT THE FIRST SUMMER AND FALL after I left the hollow working in the fruit orchards. The growers paid by the bushel, and to make any money you had to stand on a ladder all day and pick fast, but I liked being under the sun, smelling apples and peaches and pears. Most of the people around me were migrant workers from Mexico, and if they had any thoughts about how I looked, they didn't show it. I couldn't understand what they said, anyhow.

I worked my way south during the winter and picked produce in the Lakeland area down in Florida. On this one rainy spring Saturday afternoon—I was wet and trying to hitch a ride—I saw this big canvas tent in a muddy parking lot. There was a big crowd under it, and music and singing was coming out. A wooden sign said in large red letters WELCOME. It looked like a good place to dry off.

I took a seat toward the back of the tent on a metal folding chair. I had never heard such singing. The few times I'd been to church in the hollow, there was only a tinny-sounding old piano, and the people sang like they were hurting. But here a guy was playing a 'lectric guitar, and there were drums and some horns, and the singing was like from a record. The biggest surprise was that most of the people under the tent were niggers. Not redheaded half-breeds like me, but real pedigrees with skin black as coal. They were dipping and clapping with the music, and singing like I'd never heard. After about four songs they stopped, and a preacher got up, a white man, and began shouting while holding up a Bible.

"There ain't no color in the eyes of God. The Holy Spirit ain't no color. In the eyes of God it don't matter if you're white or black or green. God loves you all, the beautiful and the maimed. In heaven, everyone will be an angel, and the color of your skin is the last thing you'll be judged by."

I'd never heard that kind of talk before. Back in the hollow, and everywhere I'd gone since leaving, everything was stacked up by color. I never saw anybody but white men that owned orchards, and all the foremen were white; the Mexicans and the niggers and the mixed-up ones like me bent our backs. But here was a white man in a clean blue suit, a big gold watch on his wrist, shouting that everyone was equal. I started to feel like every word he said was spoken right to me, like I was the only person in that tent, and what that man had to say was for me only. This warm glow settled over me, and even though my clothes were still damp and a cold rain was falling outside, I could have imagined I was sitting next to a roaring fire.

People started singing again, and the preacher shouted for the sinners to come forward. I hadn't been to church enough to know if I was a bad sinner or not, but I did know I wanted to be a part of this thing where the color of your skin didn't mean nothing. Folks were crying all around me, and some of them threw their hands up and said words that didn't make sense. The next thing I knew I was coming down that aisle, and I couldn't feel my legs under me, like I was riding on air. I don't even remember what I said to that preacher, but he hugged me to his chest. A second later, I was in line with some other people, and the preacher dunked my head in a big washtub full of water. That water took my breath, and something went along my spine like I'd backed up to a hot wire. I pulled out my wallet from my front pants pocket where I kept it and gave that preacher every cent I'd saved for the past six months. A couple hundred dollars I gave him, and he hugged me again and told me my name was now in the Book of Life, and I didn't have to worry no longer about eternity. He handed me a little Bible about the size of a pack of cigarettes. When I walked out of that tent, my clothes were dry and the rain had stopped and a big moon hung in the sky.

I won't say now if it was God or good luck or maybe even bad luck that the migrant people picked me up the next morning on their way up to the Carolinas to work the tobacco season. I only say bad luck because if I hadn't stuck my thumb out at that instant, I might not be here on this mountainside with Lewis, drawing in and out of myself with a pair of burnt-out lungs. But I'd probably still be a dumb hill hick working the fields and I wouldn't have seen or done or felt the things I have these past few months. I'd lean toward good luck. I'm not sure now that God pays attention to these little things.

But that old beat-up school bus stopped and a man called to me from the window.

"You looking for work in 'baccor?"

"I'm looking for any kind of work," I answered.

"You ain't illegal, are you? You don't sound that way."

"I'm legal as a quarter," I told him.

"Climb in," he said.

I got in and found a seat toward the back of the crowded bus. Most of the people were sleeping, teenagers and grown-ups and a few younguns, nearly all of them Mexican or nigger. The air smelled of sweat and smoke. I took my little Bible and started reading real slow and tried not to worry about where I was going. We rode all day and night, stopping just to eat and gas up and use the bathroom.

I woke the next morning to see flat, sandy land with a lot of scrub oak. By noon, I was signed on to help plant my first crop of what everyone on the bus called 'baccor.

We worked the next three weeks, moving up through South Carolina following the planting season. I sat all day on a machine behind a tractor and dropped foot-long tobacco plants into the earth. The work made my back ache, and the plants gummed up my hands and smelled bad, but the pay was steady. We quit planting high in North Carolina, then followed the season south to where the tobacco plants were ready to be suckered and topped, which was pulling off the extra shoots that tried to grow out between the leaves and breaking off the yellow top flowers. Like a yo-yo, we followed the season up and down the two states, and finally got to the cropping, or what some people call priming, which was pulling off the ripe leaves.

I stayed pretty much to myself. Nights were spent sleeping on the bus between jobs or in labor camps where everyone crowded together in migrant dorms. Sometimes in the middle of the night, half the Mexicans would run off and hide in the woods till the immigration people came through and left. They'd always look me over, but as soon as I'd start talking, that Kentucky accent of mine would move them on.

I kept reading my Bible, and I found out I was invisible. People could look at me all they wanted, and they didn't see the real Elbridge Snipes. My mixed blood was only on the outside, and the real me was inside and pure as the first snow. When people stared, they might as well be looking right through me. I was a temple.

I remember good as yesterday the first time I laid eyes on Rita. She and her family rolled into camp in a rusty pickup truck. About a dozen of them climbed out of the back; she got out last. I was washing off at a spigot when she stepped down, wearing a long dress, her black hair braided into two long, thick pigtails. She was probably no more than sixteen, and she looked as delicate as a bird, as pretty as the doves I liked to shoot. Her skin was brown, her nose straight and long like my grandpa's, her eyes black as coal. I caught her eye for just a second, and though she quickly turned away, I saw a trace of a smile on her face.

We were packing the cured tobacco to take to market, and I found myself saying a word or two to her as we worked. She smelled of soap. I had liked a few girls back in the hollow, but none ever gave me a second look. I enjoyed working with the cured tobacco. I thought of it as a sort of miracle, kind of like me. You took sticky green tobacco leaves and heated them for a day with fire, and out came something that smelled good and was light in weight and the prettiest brown color. I remembered the fire that had swept down my back that night when the preacher dunked my head underwater, and how I had come out changed. There was something pure about cured tobacco, like all the sweat and backaches and cussing it took to get it out of the field was healed.

By the end of the packing season, I was talking to Rita regular. I found out she was half Indian and half Puerto Rican and was traveling with her uncle and his people. Her real folks were still on the reservation down in south Florida. Her uncle was a drinker come nighttime, as were most of the men I worked with; I noticed he had a habit of taking most of Rita's money.

One payday night toward the end of the season, I saw him slap her. I walked over close. As much as the Bible had helped me get pure, it also said an eye for an eye.

"Don't ever hit her again," I told him.

He turned and looked at me with one eye squinted. "Shut up, Red. This ain't your business."

"It's gonna be if you hit her again."

He looked back at Rita, then spun and sucker punched me on the side of my jaw. I hit him in the eye, and we fought for about ten minutes till we were both laying in the dirt.

Her uncle wiped blood from his mouth while he stared at me. Then he pulled a pint of wine from his back pocket. "You want some?" he asked.

"I don't drink."

"You want her?" he said. "You give me fifty dollars and she can go with you."

Rita and I locked eyes. She nodded once, and I pulled out my wallet.

We got married the next day, by the judge in Clinton.

I didn't have much money left, but there was enough to get us a room at the Econo Lodge. I was scared of what I knew was supposed to happen now, my stomach all nervous. We went over to the Wal-Mart to get a few things, then had our first married meal at Shoney's. It was barely dark when we were back at the room, and my belly was twisted tight.

"Why don't you go wash up," Rita said.

I took a long shower, surprised that the water didn't go cold. There were little bars of soap and clean towels in the bathroom. I brushed my teeth real good, something I had started doing since reading the Bible and realizing my body was a temple. I put my clothes back on, and then she went, and I sat on the bed and stared at the blank television screen. I got up and turned on the air conditioner and put my face against that good cold air. I couldn't believe how long she stayed in the bathroom, but finally the door opened, and Rita reached and flipped off the overhead light.

I could see just her outline against the mirror, the light from the bathroom behind her. She had on a long silky gown, and I could make out her legs through it. I smelled her perfume as she walked toward me. I was afraid I would vomit.

What happened next is kind of a blur, but I remember her lips against mine, and thinking that was the best thing I'd ever felt. I didn't know about sex except for a few magazines I'd looked at and some jokes I'd heard. I had seen a lot of animals bred, so I knew what had to be done. Rita started pulling off my clothes and kissing me in places I'd never dreamed of. I knew I couldn't last much longer.

"Turn around," I told her.

"What?" she asked.

"You know. Turn around so I can put it in." I was glad the room was dark.

She laughed real softly and rolled on her back, then pulled me on top of her. I guess she'd had some practice. We were up most of the night.

The next three years were the best of my life. I got hired on as permanent help by Mr. Bill Turner, who owned a five-hundred-acre farm that grew tobacco and beans and corn. The job came with a little tenant house and a garden plot. The house wasn't fancy, had an out-house and a hand water-pump, but it was dry and warm. I saved enough money to buy a used car. At the Methodist church we attended down the road, some of the people looked at me and Rita kind of strange, but they didn't say anything. I studied my Bible at night and knew that on the inside I was perfect and pure. Cindy was born eleven months after we were married, and Connie followed her a year later.

We grew a big garden in the summer and had a collard and turnip patch in the winter. I kept some chickens in a pen and raised a hog each year to slaughter. I shot doves and quail during their seasons. We lived pretty much off the lan', like my grandpa used to say. I think I could have stayed on the farm the rest of my life.

The drought started one spring right when me and Turner were planting corn and beans. Six weeks passed without a drop of rain, and the ground was dry as dust. I prayed every night for rain, and it came close to us at times, yet somehow always missed our fields. In May we started setting out tobacco plants. The corn and beans were already pretty much a loss. I could see the worry lines in Turner's face. We were able to irrigate the tobacco, and it was growing pretty good despite the weather. Finally there was a big thunderstorm, but it brought hail with it and riddled about a third of the crop.

The migrant help came in their buses and trucks in early July to crop the tobacco. I didn't have to bend my back any longer; instead I drove a tractor and made sure everyone worked and pulled ripe leaves. I got cussed at a lot behind my back 'cause I was the boss, but being called a son of a bitch or a half-breed in Spanish ain't the same as being called it in English. The second cropping came off good, and we filled three barns in two days and fired them.

Midnight had come and gone one night, and I was sleeping, when Rita pulled on my shoulder and woke me up. From the bedroom window I could see a red glow. I jumped up and looked out toward the barns and saw fire coming through the roof of the middle one. I was at Turner's house within three minutes, pounding on the door. When me and him got to the fire, there wasn't a thing to do but stand back and look. A burning tobacco barn is like a match going off. Just before the fire truck arrived, the propane gas tank exploded and the fire jumped to the other two barns, and all three burned to the ground. I remember Turner's face, the fire shining on it, making the lines around his eyes stand out like cuts. I had this sour feeling in my stomach. I guess now that fire was an omen. Turner had to file for bankruptcy in the fall, and though he said he hated to, he had to let me go.

Flames

Lewis

I FEEL RIGHT NOW like I'm in the center of the universe, as if everything is revolving around me; I'm the hub, and spokes are coming out of me shaped like trees and mountains, and the moon and stars are floating on the rim. The sky keeps turning above me, and stars rise above the mountains.

An owl hoots in the woods, and the breeze whispers in the tree branches. I could swear sometimes I hear voices. Elbridge has been quiet for the last hour, breathing slow. I want him to keep on breathing at least till the sun comes up. I wouldn't want him to die with the dark all around him. I want him to see the light on the mountains.

The air is cold, but I feel pretty warm with him close to me. Mars has climbed above the mountains; it's there against the sky as red as an ember. The god of war, Mars is, and I know about fighting. I've raged and hated so much over the past year that I came to believe anger was the only emotion left. But it has all drained from me like water down a sink, and what is in me now is something I can't explain. I'm filled with nothing but air, and waiting for something new to flow inside me. I don't know where the anger went, but it's left me, and I'm sitting here in the dark with a dying man, watching the world turn.

My whole life I've been watching my flank and backside, waiting to tackle whatever was coming at me. Doing battle, I learned the rules early; I learned to play by them, and how far I could bend them without getting caught. I know now it was all a game, and the rules for one man ain't necessarily the rules for another. There was a warrior I knew once, and he played the game hard and stayed within the rules. I knew him so long ago he is like an old black-and-white movie in my memory.

Everything that mattered in the universe was contained in Kenan Stadium. The roar of sixty thousand standing fans fell on the ball field like an avalanche. The November sky was clear and cold and blue, the playing field trampled and torn under cleated feet that had battled to an almost even score. Lewis looked up into the mass of screaming faces and wished he could single out Beverly's amid the thousands. He glanced again at the scoreboard. Carolina 27, State 24; three seconds left on the clock; third and goal on the two yard line. He waved the blue-helmeted defense together into a huddle.

"The fuckers are going for it," Lewis shouted. "Are we tougher? Are we going to stop their asses?"

"Hell, yeah!" his teammates answered.

"We're Carolina, God damn it. We're harder than a brick wall. You hear me? Harder than a brick fucking wall. Blitz. Tommy, red-dog the corner. I'm coming through the deuce hole."

The defense clasped hands, then broke apart. The big linesmen got in their trench, butts up and heads down.

Lewis stood splay-legged and crouched at his linebacker position behind them. The noise was tactile, like heavy rain falling. State's offense lined up, and the quarter-back's head swept left, then right.

They're going to run it, Lewis thought. Right down the middle. Come on and try it. Try it, motherfuckers. He admired them for going for the win. A field goal would tie the game, but a tie wasn't a win.

Lewis, six-foot-four, two hundred twenty-five pounds of bone and muscle, was playing his senior year as middle linebacker and co-captain for the University of North Carolina Tar Heels. The chalk goal line at his feet was his property, and nobody was taking it from him. He had learned how you kept people from taking things from you. You rammed your elbow through their gut and said no.

State's quarterback studied the defense, and then crouched behind his center. "Sixteen," he yelled.

Lewis placed the knuckles of his right hand against the grass.

His old man had watched football on television every Sunday afternoon, downing six-packs during the games. Lewis usually watched with him, but his allegiance was more to his father than to the game. Footballs had appeared on his bed after whiskey drunks, but they mostly collected dust in a closet.

A few days into his freshman year in high school, as Lewis stood at his locker getting his biology book, he felt something sharp strike his shoulder. He slapped at the hurt and looked around. Muffled laughter came from a cluster of boys nearby. Lewis turned again to his locker. A second pain hit him in the back of the neck, as hot as a wasp sting. He slapped his neck and felt a spot of blood, then grasped a large paper clip under his collar. He whirled around at another fit of laughter.

Jerry, the oldest of Mrs. Bullard's sons, stood across the hallway with his friends, a big smirk on his face. Lewis stared at the paper clip in his palm. He knew the game. You bent a paper clip double and shot it with a rubber band, like an arrow. He felt blood trickle down his neck.

"You better not do that again," he said, tightening his jaw against his rage and pain.

"Do what, orphan?" Jerry's eyes were wide with feigned innocence.

"Hit me with a paper clip. That's what."

Jerry cackled. "I didn't hit you. That was probably one of your cooties biting you." He nudged one of his friends, and they both laughed.

Jerry had picked on Lewis since he had first come to stay with the Bullards. Jerry had always been bigger, and he pinched and shoved the younger boy and blamed every accident on him.

"I don't have cooties," Lewis said.

"You used to. Mom had to wash you with dog shampoo."

Lewis's face burned as several other students stopped and listened to the argument. On one of his visits a few years before, Mrs. Bullard had seen lice crawling on his collar. An inspection of his hair revealed why his scalp had been so itchy for a week.

"Don't you ever bathe?" she had questioned. "Don't you ever use soap and water?"

"Yes, ma'am. I got the lice at school. A lot of kids—"

"I know how you got them. You got them from that

filthy house you live in with that filthy father of yours. Well, you're fixing to get a bath. You're not bringing lice into my house."

She had made Lewis take a bath with dog shampoo. The strong soap burned his scalp worse than the lice did. Jerry had watched and laughed from the bathroom doorway.

"Hey, where'd you steal those sneakers from?" Jerry shouted at him now.

Before school opened, Lewis had used some of his tobacco money on a pair of Nikes. "I didn't steal them," he answered. "I bought them."

"Where'd you get money? You used to always wear my hand-me-downs. Hand-me-down clothes and head lice. The kid is a real winner."

A dozen students were watching now. Lewis looked Jerry in the eye. "Don't hit me again." He turned again to his locker.

"Shut up, orphan," Jerry yelled, and Lewis felt another paper clip strike him in the center of the back. The hallway went silent. Lewis whirled around. That same smirk filled Jerry's face—the expression Lewis had endured for years. Something ignited inside him. He crossed the hallway in three long strides and, before Jerry's smirk had time to fade, rammed his head into his tormentor's gut. He pushed with his calves, as he had seen football linesmen on television do, and kept driving forward until Jerry smashed against the wall. Lewis stood with his fist balled, and the smirk disappeared from Jerry's face as he gasped for breath. He slid down the wall, his mouth opening and closing like that of a bream pulled from water. Instantly, a teacher grasped Lewis's arm and led him to the principal's office.

"You know it's automatic suspension for fighting?" Mr. James said after closing the door to his office.

"Yes, sir." Lewis stood straight like a soldier.

"Who started the fight?"

"He—I guess we both did, sir."

The principal pursed his lips and walked around Lewis in a slow circle. "You're getting big, son. You're quite a few inches taller than you were last year."

"Yes, sir."

Mr. James stopped in front of Lewis. "I knew your dad, son. We went to school together."

Lewis glanced at the principal.

"Has your father told you about when he played football?"

"No, sir. But he watches a lot of football."

"Well, you should ask him about when he played. We were on the junior varsity together. Your dad was by far the best on the team. He would have been the best on the varsity if he hadn't quit school to work."

"I didn't know that, sir."

Mr. James sat down in his chair. "Why aren't you playing football? You're big. You got your father's blood in you."

"I never thought about it much. I was cropping tobacco when tryouts started."

"Well, you should think about it. In fact, instead of suspending you, I think I'll make you play ball. We need to redirect that energy of yours."

"Sir, tryouts are already over."

"Oh, the coach could still use a big, strapping boy like you." Mr. James picked up the phone.

Midway through his sophomore year, Lewis had passed six feet and was starting for the varsity team. By his senior year, the kid who had been teased throughout grammar school because of his shabby clothes had become the school hero. His father, sober or not, attended all the home games. Not long after Lewis and his team won the state championship that year, the old man died of a heart attack while plumbing underneath a house.

"Nine," State's quarterback called out. "Seventeen." Lewis watched the quarterback's eyes. Words meant nothing: the flick of his eyes, the slight nod of his head were the signals to look for. The offensive end went into motion. Another deception. They weren't going to pass, they were going to try running through the middle, and Lewis owned the middle. His leg muscles were coiled as tight as steel, ready to burst at the snap.

This is for you, baby girl, he thought. For you, Bev.

"Forty-four," the quarterback yelled. The crowd's roar was like the world caving in.

Honeysuckle perfumed the air, and the sun shone on daffodils growing in yellow-and-green clumps beneath the trees. Lewis and Beverly walked a path above the river.

"This is even more beautiful than I thought it could be," Beverly said. "You were right. I love it."

She curled her arms above her head and spun like a ballerina. Her dress swirled high on her legs, and her long red hair swung in a plume. Lewis smiled. She was, he thought, the most beautiful girl in the world, with her slender figure, green eyes, and spattering of freckles. Beverly was like a blossom to him, fragile and simple. She favored jeans or dresses, often put her hair in braids, and wore very little makeup.

She bent and slipped off her sandals. "Take your shoes off. The ground feels wonderful."

He shook his head. "I can't afford a stone bruise. I've been doing a lot of running lately."

"Sissy."

They had met in economics class. He had asked to borrow a pencil to take notes, and they'd exchanged names. He blushed when she said she'd seen him play ball. They'd been out for pizza twice; he'd kissed her good night the second time, but today was the first they'd been alone. Lewis's stomach fluttered.

He was at the end of his junior year, and had made second team all-ACC. The grueling weight training and practice and running had paid off: he had developed into a rock-hard linebacker and been elected team co-captain. Lewis had a wide choice of girls to date, but he'd found that most of them wanted to bed down the first time they went out. Despite all the attention now, the years of being laughed at had not been erased.

"It's down there." Lewis pointed to a small grassy clearing beside the water. "Watch the trail. It's kind of steep."

"Hold my hand?" Beverly said.

They reached the clearing, and Beverly took a blanket out of her woven basket and spread it on the ground. They sat down. Water murmured from between rocks that emerged above the current.

"How'd you ever find this place?" she asked. "It's so quiet."

"Just found it. I do a lot of walking in the woods when I can. I grew up in the sticks, you know. It's in my blood."

"I wish I had," Beverly said softly. She was the only

daughter of wealthy parents in the tobacco business in Winston-Salem. "Most of the trees I saw were in city parks."

She leaned against him, and he put his arm around her shoulder and felt his heart quicken. With her finger, she traced small circles on his pants leg.

"What do you want out of life?" she asked.

He chuckled. "That's the big question."

"Are you going to play professional?"

"I guess. If I can make it. I get kind of tired of knocking heads, though."

"What do you really want to do?"

He sighed, then lay back on the blanket. Beverly rested her chin on his chest. "Build. I've had about enough of knocking stuff down."

"Build what?"

"Houses. I learned a lot about carpentry when I was growing up. I remember the old man saying, 'Son, don't be a plumber. You'll always have your face in the dirt. Be the one who hires the plumber.' So I'd like to be a contractor."

As they listened in silence to the water, a male mallard swooped low over the river. At the sight of them, it took wing.

"What do you want to do?" Lewis asked.

Beverly turned her head and rested her cheek against his chest. She closed her eyes for a moment. "Teach fifth grade."

"That should be easy enough," he answered. "You have a four-point-oh."

"Yes, but Mother wants me to do a lot more. She wants me to go to graduate school and go on for a Ph.D."

"That's ambitious."

"It's ridiculous. I want to teach children, not a bunch of pampered college kids." She sat up and spread her arms wide. "I feel so free out here. Just me and you and the song of the water and wind." She rolled to her back on the blanket, her eyes closed, a smile brightening her face. "This place is so sexy," she said. "I feel spring flowing in my blood."

Lewis's heart thumped. She was beautiful lying there, a rich girl who didn't wear makeup and who wanted to teach children, on her back in the sun by the river.

Beverly reached up and clasped her arms around his neck. Her dress had slid high on her long legs. Lewis swallowed coarsely, then moved his lips to hers. She smelled of perfume and perspiration.

The sound of splashing water made him draw back from her. He turned and saw three does and a buck bounding across the shallow water downstream.

"What was that?" Beverly asked.

"Deer. Something spooked them. Must be a fisherman or something."

He stood and pulled Beverly to her feet. "We better go."

She held her lips in a pretended pout. "Can we come here again?"

"We'll come, sure." He nodded. "We'll come again another time."

"Hut! Hut!" State's quarterback dipped his head just a fraction of an inch, but that was enough for Lewis to know the snap was coming. The ball had barely moved when he exploded off the line, his legs launching him like catapults. The universe was only noise and color, the slamming of shoulder pads and grunts and shouts, the crowd in the stadium standing and screaming.

Lewis followed the left tackle, and when the deuce hole opened, he came through it like a battering ram. The quarterback was still pedaling in reverse, turning to his right for the handoff, the fullback in motion. Lewis jigged to avoid the halfback's block, lowered his head, and put it into the fullback's gut as soon as he took the ball. Lewis had the momentum, and he slammed his opponent backward; his arms wrapped around the player's waist as he brought him down.

The pistol cracked, and the game was over. Lewis's teammates pounded him to the earth, slapping his helmet and shouting. The crowd roared and spilled onto the field, the band belted out the victory song. Lewis exchanged high fives, all the time searching the crowd; finally he saw Beverly wedging her way through. She ran to him, and he caught her under the arms as she scissored him.

She dotted his forehead and cheeks with kisses. "I love you," she yelled.

"Let's get married."

Her eyes widened, and her mouth opened. "What did you say?"

"I said, 'Let's get married'!"

Lewis carried her off the field in his arms like a doll, her face buried against his neck, her happy tears mixing with the salt of battle.

Inferno

THE SILVER EYE OF NIGHT rose higher and higher above the two huddled men. The light was splintered by high ice crystals, and a halo had formed around the moon. Frost coating the grass and trees caught the moonglow, and they shone with their own cold fire. A rabbit searching for morsels of food was nearly upon the two men before it scented them and turned and scurried into the brush. The night grew stiller, the only sounds the whisper of wind and the occasional whine of jets as they lifted from the airport and headed over the mountains for points distant. In the top of a spruce sat an owl, its yellow eyes searching the meadow for field mice. "Who, who?" it called, wary of the dark mass against the rock.

Lewis

WHO AM I? That owl seems to want to know. I don't really have an answer. I've been so many people in these last years—a child, a warrior, a man, a husband and father, a snake. But just as snakes shed their skins and crawl out of them, I feel I've been reborn, and I don't know which of the people and beasts I used to be still exist.

I've been thinking about what it means to be a man. For a year now I've tried to blot out those thoughts with vodka while traveling as far as I could from my memories of people and places. I think now that manhood is more a definition than a title. My father always told me that men don't cry. I never saw him drop a tear, not once; instead of spilling water, he poured beer and whiskey down his throat—sort of like crying in reverse. This fellow I'm holding, I've seen him cry plenty, but I'm coming to think he's also about as much a man as I've seen. He ain't very big, but he stood up against the very thing that knocked me flat on my ass. Like father, like son: I never was one to cry. They say a person is about ninety-five percent water, and I felt that each time you cried you were losing a part of your body. I knew a man once who lived by that creed, but he is long deceased, like the dinosaurs.

That's not the one, Lewis thought as he watched the young deer take hesitant steps into the clearing, ears pointed and nostrils flared. He ain't the one, no way.

Lewis had been in the tree stand since dawn, watching the sun add color to the world, waiting for the big buck he had been scouting for two months. He'd seen the buck's signs—rubs on small trees where the bark had been peeled away, scrapes where the buck had pawed the forest floor and pissed to mark his territory, big turds the animal had left. He was an old, smart deer, probably weighing two hundred pounds and carrying a rack of at least ten points. The young buck Lewis studied might have been one of his offspring.

Several does followed the young male to the river's edge, where they lowered their muzzles and drank. The big buck never showed, the sun inched higher in the tree branches, but Lewis remained in the stand, enjoying the first true peace he had felt in weeks. Since the birth of the baby, he and Beverly had been arguing more and more over matters they once would have deemed trivial. The realities of life had caught up with them, the dreams and innocent ideals of youth squashed under the demands and pressures of being parents and adults. A quarrel could begin over Lewis's leaving his boots in the middle of the bedroom floor or forgetting to call when he was going to be home late from work. Beverly seemed unable to understand how much time and energy it took to run a construction company, and Lewis resented the many hours she devoted to her own concerns.

Finally Lewis could not ignore the time any longer. He climbed down from the tree and walked to his truck.

A lone dove dipped and darted against the sky beyond the windshield of the Chevy Blazer as Lewis drove off. He watched the bird until it lifted over the treetops and disappeared. He envied the dove's freedom: not tied to clocks and bank mortgages and marital vows, the bird lived one with the wind, its only boundaries the clouds and the soil.

Lewis swung into the drive-through at Hardee's and ordered a breakfast of steak biscuits and coffee before heading for the construction site, a subdivision that was being cut out of a forest tract on the outskirts of Chapel Hill. When he turned onto the new asphalt road of the development, he saw the stud walls of a two-story house, only one of several homes in various stages of construction under his supervision. The carpenters inside made him think of a bunch of Jonahs in the ribs of the whale. He heard the rapid fire of framing hammers, the high whine of a ripsaw. Within six weeks a family would be living there.

"Boss man," Pete, the crew foreman, called from inside the house. He had worked for Lewis for five years, since the start of his company. Lewis reached for his clipboard as he stepped from the truck. Pete met him at the front steps. "See anything?"

"Just a little one."

"Little, my ass. I bet it was a ten-pointer. Now where'd you say your stand is at?"

"In the woods." Lewis and Pete and several friends had set a wager each year on who could kill the biggest buck. The competition was good-natured but fierce. "How's everything going?"

"We're smoking. Ought to finish framing today and be ready to start the rafters Monday."

"I'll make sure Fitch delivers more wood this afternoon."

Lewis studied his five carpenters, their arms a blur as they swung twenty-two-ounce framing hammers. He watched the new worker he had hired a few days before—part of a program at a homeless shelter. Beverly had talked him into it. The fellow looked about fifty, eyes washed out, clothes old and ragged. His shirt was dark with sweat.

"How's the new guy doing?"

Pete raked his top teeth over his bottom lip. " 'Bout what you'd expect from that place. He bends more nails than he sinks."

CURED BY FIRE / 81

"Watch him close today. I told him I'd try him for a week."

"But he's *homeless*!" Pete exclaimed in mock concern.

Lewis walked through the house, stopping occasionally to take the tape measure from his belt and note the width of a board or a window space. He had learned not to trust anyone completely with anything. Level and plumb: that's how the foundation and walls of a house had to be. You had to start out solid and square, and if you did, any small mistakes could, in the long run, be hidden in the trim work.

"I'm making the rounds," Lewis told Pete when he was satisfied with the inspection. "Yeah, try and get through with the framing today."

"Right on, boss." Pete snapped to and saluted.

"Making the rounds" meant seeing a multitude of building supply agents, lawyers, county inspectors, surveyors, and customers, chewing the fat and shaking hands, playing either the businessman or the good ol' boy, depending on the person he was seeing. Lewis played at life as he had played ball: act and react on instinct, dodge, bluff, lie back, knock 'em down.

By three o'clock, after the many meetings, and lunch from Wendy's eaten between stops, Lewis was back in the driveway of the house under construction. He buckled on a carpenter's belt and joined the crew, driving sixteen-penny nails in like a machine—one tap to set each nail, two solid bangs to seat it. The hammering sounded like a small war.

It was around five when the last wall was lifted and nailed. The house was now solid as rock. Lewis called Pete over.

"How'd the new guy do?"

Pete frowned. "He ain't a carpenter. He's a charity case."

Lewis nodded, then turned and walked toward his truck. He opened the tailgate and placed the big Igloo cooler, always filled with cold beer on Fridays, on the ground. The workmen crowded around, lifted cans and popped them open. From the cab, Lewis took his ledger with the previous week's paychecks. He tore them from the book and called out names.

"Hey, bud," Lewis said to his newest worker, "I need to talk to you for a second." They went to the front of the truck while the other men concentrated on a joke Pete had started.

"I'm gonna have to let you go," Lewis began. "This framing work is a little rough for an older man."

"I—I was getting the hang of it, sir. I can do better."

"No. Remember I said I'd give you a try. This is hard work for even a young man."

"I need the work, sir."

Lewis stared at the house and shook his head. "I can't keep you on here. Look, I know some people who might have a job for you, washing dishes or something."

The man took a deep breath. "Do I get a check?"

"Checks are held back a week. You can stop by next Friday."

"I don't have no money."

Lewis sighed. He removed his wallet from his pocket, thumbed through it, pulled out a twenty, hesitated, then pulled out another. "Here, I'll advance you a little."

The man looked none too pleased. He grabbed the money all the same, and walked away quickly.

The crew was still laughing at Pete's joke when Lewis joined them.

"T.G.I.F.," Pete said. He reached for a beer and

handed it to Lewis, who popped it open and drank half without stopping.

"Don't look so blue, boss man," Pete told him. "Hell, them bleeding hearts down on Franklin Street will fill his pocket with quarters."

Lewis smiled weakly. "Yeah, you're right about that." He finished his beer, then reached for another can from the cooler. The beer was cold and went down easy, and it tasted especially good after a long week. He figured the crew thought likewise.

"Hey, how about y'all cleaning up the cooler," he said.

"Right-o, boss man," Pete answered. "I believe we can take care of this little ol' cooler. But wait a minute— ain't you gonna tell me where your deer stand is?"

"Sure thing." Lewis grinned. "Like I said, it's in the woods."

Lewis drank another beer on the way to his office. By now, a good tingle had begun in his forehead, and some of the tension of work was loosening. The construction business was a juggling act—there was always cash flow to deal with, and bills—but Lewis usually managed to stay a week ahead of the bank. Like other folks, he had to earn his pay; social problems were for the government to worry about; even the so-called homeless should have to pull their weight. Lewis had a two-year-old and a wife to support, a mortgage to pay, a business to operate. Often late at night when he wasn't able to sleep he wondered why life had to get so complicated. At one time he had had just himself to think about; he could put his head down and shove forward over his problems. Now he had to talk and shake hands and bullshit with the best of them to stay in the race.

He tossed the empty can on the floorboard, got out of

the truck, and walked toward a two-story office complex. At the glass door he paused and combed his hair against his reflection. He entered and proceeded down the hall, then opened the door of Tar Heel Contractors.

A pretty young woman looked up from her desk and smiled broadly at him. "Hello, Mr. Calhoon. How was your day, sir?"

"Cut the crap, Rachel," Lewis said, his own smile equally broad. "Until eight o'clock Monday morning I am not a Mister or a sir."

"Well, Lewis, how was your day, honey chil'?"

"Hell, as usual. Didn't see a decent deer this morning."

"What sort were you looking for?" She arched one eyebrow. "D-E-E-R or D-E-A-R?"

"The type with antlers, that doesn't talk. I have the other type at home."

"She called this afternoon. Wanted to know if I knew what time you'd be home."

"Who else called?"

"About a dozen people. I put the messages on your desk."

Lewis shook his head. "Jesus Christ." He walked into an adjoining room and closed the door. He took a beer from the mini-refrigerator, and sat at his desk and swigged from it while he sorted through papers. As he wrote the names and numbers he needed to phone on Monday in his calendar, there was a soft knock on the door.

"Come in."

Rachel stuck her head and shoulders through the doorway. "I'm going to leave now, if you don't need me for anything."

"I'm about through here. You go ahead."

"Tell Beverly hello."

Lewis nodded. He admired the slope of Rachel's shoulders that showed under the neck of her peasant blouse. "You have a good weekend."

"You too. Behave yourself!"

Lewis stared at the door for several seconds after Rachel was gone. He had hired her six months before, when he'd opened his first real office. She was a golden-haired, green-eyed twenty-five-year-old who always wore lacy dresses that swished about her bare legs. She had confided in him a few weeks back that she was having problems with her husband. Lewis wanted to call to her now, and ask her to come in and sit down and have a beer with him. Instead, he filled his mouth with another swallow of beer.

The Pine Knoll subdivision, one of the older developments in Chapel Hill, consisted mostly of ranch-style houses on one-acre lots with plenty of oak and hickory trees—more modest constructions than the two- and three-story mansions that he and his crew built. Like most of the subdivisions around town, Pine Knoll was filled with middle-class white people with college degrees.

He wheeled into the driveway of a brick three-bedroom with a deck out back. Here was refuge from the business war he fought every day. Inside were a baby girl and a wife he loved, a color television and a good stereo, and a refrigerator stocked with food. The house was a mountain range separating Lewis from his childhood. He owned it and he'd be damned if he'd lose it.

After their honeymoon in Florida, Lewis and Beverly had returned to Chapel Hill. Home then was a small one-bedroom rental on a quiet street close to campus. Lewis had lifted Beverly into his arms at the door, and carried her over the threshold and straight to the bedroom.

The next morning, he rose early and slipped from bed, being careful not to wake Beverly. He washed the sleep from his eyes with cold water, then walked slowly through the house. The walls needed a fresh coat of paint, the living room carpet was faded, all the furniture had seen years of use. But the house was clean and had a fenced backyard. He was excited here in a way he never had been before: this was the very first dwelling where he felt he held life in his hands, and it trembled and throbbed like a nestling bird.

Lewis went into the kitchen, took a saucepan and a skillet from the cupboard, and eggs and bacon from the refrigerator. His thoughts were elsewhere as he watched grease melt in the pan. He'd managed to save some money from a short stint with the Cowboys the past summer, and he'd hired two guys with experience in carpentry. The Rams' Club at the university had agreed to help him contract jobs, and three had already been lined up, to build decks on some of the alumni's houses. He'd opened an account at Fitch's Lumber so he could charge tools and material and pay at the end of jobs. The president of a local bank, a football fan, had offered him an unsecured loan upon demand.

Lewis put his mind to breakfast. He made grits to go with the fried eggs and bacon, buttered some toast and brewed a pot of coffee. He plucked a red rose from the backyard, and put it in an empty soda bottle. With the flower and breakfast on a tray, he tiptoed to the bedroom, where Beverly still slept.

"Wake up, sleepy-head." Lewis set the tray on the

dresser, then walked to the bed and gently squeezed Beverly's shoulder. "Hey, lady. This ain't Disney World any longer. Rise and shine."

Beverly mumbled and opened her eyes. She sat up and glanced around the room, looking confused. "Oh, Lewis! I didn't know where I was at first."

"You're home sweet home. I made you breakfast."

"I was so exhausted. I slept like a baby."

"That's because you are a baby. My baby." He leaned to kiss her.

Beverly clasped her hand over her mouth. "Wait. I've got morning breath," she said between her fingers.

"I don't care." He kissed her knuckles. "Now sit up straight. I'm your waiter."

"You're so sweet. I was planning to cook *you* breakfast."

"The early bird gets the frying pan. Besides, you needed your beauty sleep."

Lewis adjusted the pillow behind her back and carefully placed the tray on her lap. With an exaggerated gesture, he tucked a paper towel over the neckline of her nightgown. Beverly giggled. He fed her bites of bacon and eggs until she made him stop.

"You remember Mother and Father are coming for lunch?"

Lewis nodded. He wished they would wait at least a week, but didn't say so.

"Let's take them to Dip's." Beverly lifted her coffee cup and sipped from it. A smile brightened her face. "I had the best dream last night."

"A wet dream?"

She playfully slapped his hand. "It was like a fairy tale. We were in this big house, and there were flowers in vases all over the room. The floor was made of clouds. We were standing on clouds. And the colors! The colors were brilliant. It was the most peaceful feeling. Like we were angels living in a castle.''

Lewis laughed. "You were at Disney World too long."

"But it seemed so real, baby. I had this wonderful, wonderful feeling."

"Well, baby girl, we're in a castle right now. I'm the king and you're the queen, and we rule this world. Remember that ride at Disney, It's a Small, Small World? Remember sailing over those little towns? That's how I feel right now. We have the whole world in the palm of our hands."

He bent toward Beverly, and this time she let him kiss her lips.

Beverly's parents knocked on the front door a few minutes after noon. Mr. Anderson was trim and graying; his wife was well preserved, with the good looks of her daughter. They had always been cordial toward Lewis, but wished their only child had fallen in love with someone whose talents involved something more refined than crushing quarterbacks and pounding nails.

After the hugs and handshakes, Beverly led the way inside. "Isn't this the cutest place!" she exclaimed. "Lewis found it at the last minute."

Mrs. Anderson scanned the small living room. "Oh, it's cute, all right."

"We've got some fixing up to do," Lewis said. "I'm going to paint the interior first."

"I'm going to help." Beverly held Lewis's arm.

"Yes, I think a coat of paint would be a good beginning," Mrs. Anderson replied.

Over lunch, at an upscale restaurant that served southern cuisine, Mr. Anderson quizzed his son-in-law. "So what's the game plan now, to use one of your terms, Lewis? Are you still going with your construction company?"

"Well, I wouldn't exactly call it a 'construction company' yet. But I've hired two guys, and we have some jobs lined up."

"What sort of jobs?"

"Right now just small stuff. Decks. I figure when the weather starts getting cold, I'll try to get some interior work trimming out houses."

"Don't you intend to use your degree?" Mrs. Anderson asked.

Lewis hunched his shoulders. "Well, I still need nine hours to finish. Besides, the field of sports psychology isn't exactly on fire these days."

"Lewis is going to night school to finish his degree, Mother," Beverly said in defense.

Mr. Anderson took a sip from his glass of tea. "Have you ever thought about going to engineering school? I have some connections up at UV."

"I've considered it," Lewis lied. "Maybe on down the line. But for now, there's a lot of money to be made around here. Chapel Hill is really growing."

"Mother," Beverly changed the subject, "I'm going to begin substituting in the fall."

"Well, dear, that's nice, but I would much rather see you studying to be a professor than herding children around all day."

"It's only temporary. And I want some time to be with Lewis."

When the check came, Mr. Anderson covered it with his hand.

"I'd like to pay," Lewis said.

"No, no. I'll get it. You save your money for paint."

"Sir, I have *plenty* of money, for the meal and the paint."

Lewis felt Beverly's hand on his knee. Mr. Anderson waved for the waitress and handed her the bill and his American Express card. Lewis flipped a twenty-dollar bill on the table, knowing it was much too big a tip.

Beverly's parents stayed only an hour after lunch. Lewis watched from the window as she accompanied them to their car. He saw Mr. Anderson's mouth moving and Mrs. Anderson nodding. Beverly shook her head. Her father pulled her to him and hugged her, then put a piece of paper in her hand and closed her fingers around it.

"What did he give you?" Lewis asked when Beverly came inside.

She smiled, but her face looked strained. "Just a check."

"For what?"

Beverly sighed. "Mother wants us to rent a bigger place."

"You don't like this house, Bev?"

"I love it, honey. You know how Mother and Father are."

"How much did he give you?"

Beverly hesitated, then handed him the check. "It's only a loan. They just want to help us."

Lewis stared at the check, made out to Beverly: five hundred dollars.

"It's just a loan, Lewis."

"No, it's more than that, baby. It's more than a loan. It's a debt."

*

Everything was relative, Lewis mused as he parked his truck. The apartment they had later moved into had seemed grand compared to the little house, and the brick ranch-style he looked at now was like a castle compared with the shack where he'd grown up. One day he'd be putting up the walls for their own big place in the country, a place like those he built for other people now.

Lewis collected the mail from the mailbox and picked up the morning paper still lying on the gravel. He entered the house, dumped the paper and the mail on a table, and walked straight into the living room, where Lillian sat surrounded by dolls. She smiled at the sight of her father, who bent and picked her up. "I'm home, Bev," he called out, then said softly, "Hey, Lilly girl. How's my darling?"

The child had her father's dark eyes and black hair, her mother's fair skin and petite mouth and nose. Lewis cradled her in his arms and swung her back and forth. He lifted the front of her frilly dress and buzzed her belly with his lips. She giggled.

Beverly appeared in the doorway. She had cut her mane of red hair when Lillian was born, and her freckles were now muted behind makeup. "Lewis," she scolded. "Put her down until you wash your hands."

"A little dirt will make her grow."

"She's growing right on schedule." Beverly kissed him lightly on the lips. She wore a navy dress suit with shoulder pads.

"Why're you so dressed up?"

"Because we're going out."

Lewis wrinkled his forehead. "What?"

"Dirk and Helen want us to meet them at Crook's for

dinner. I've been busy with the fund-raiser and haven't had time to think about cooking. I've called Mabel."

"Baby, I'm tired. Let's just stay in and order a pizza."

"Please, Lewis. All you ever do is work. I need to talk to Helen about the fund-raiser."

"Ask them to come over here for pizza."

Beverly took Lillian from his arms. "You old stick-in-the-mud." She was smiling, but her words carried an edge. "What happened to that romancer I married? Now scoot. Go get washed up. You smell like a horse."

Lewis opened his mouth to protest, but realized that more words would only lead to an argument. He went into the kitchen and took a beer out of the refrigerator, then went to bathe.

Elbridge

I'VE FLOATED OUT AGAIN. I'm like the ocean, surging forward and being sucked back, in and out of myself. I hear this hum in the air, like someone plucked a giant guitar string and the noise is almost gone. Just a low hum, a nice sound, kind of like the wind and running water mixed together. I keep thinking I see shapes in the sky. I can't make them out, but there are forms that move and blend with the blackness beyond the stars.

Lewis must be sleeping. His eye is closed and his breath is regular. He's a big man. He'd make two of me. I don't believe I ever saw a man that was hurt so bad on the outside and still breathing. He's hurt even worse on the inside. I wish I could give him some of this peace I feel right now. I can't explain it, but it's like there's a word on the tip of my tongue, and that one word explains everything in the world, in the whole sky. If I knew that word and could speak it to Lewis, maybe his wounds would heal. The word won't come to me, not yet. But something is coming. Each time I slip out of myself, the sky seems a little closer and that hum I hear is a little louder, and now I see those shapes moving behind the moon and the stars.

One thing I do know is that I been wrong about a lot of stuff. For a while there I got caught up in those words about being a temple. I liked to think about myself as something inside and not worry anymore about what anybody thought about me on the outside. I kept that temple locked up. But a temple has got to have doors, or else it's no better than a prison. If you take those words about the temple too strong, that's what you'll become, shut up inside a prison, thinking all the time you're sitting inside a temple. And another thing I know is that it ain't no sin to put your arms around a person if they need it. The sin is if a person lifts their arms to you, and you turn your back and walk away.

My old car went out after we left the farm in Clinton and had just crossed the mountains into Tennessee. I was hoping to catch work with the apple crop before the season ended. We were loaded down with everything we owned, which really was only about enough to fill up the trunk, mostly clothes and a TV and my shotgun, which I had managed to hold on to through all those miles and months. The younguns were fussing and crying, and Rita stared through the window like she wanted to shut out the whole world. I stood against the car beside the highway until a state patrolman stopped. He checked my license and registration, asked some questions, and told me he'd have a wrecker sent.

The man at the service station said the car had thrown a rod, whatever that was, and it took four hundred dollars to fix it, which was about half the money I'd saved over the three years on the farm. We drove into Bristol, Tennessee, on a Monday morning. I asked a man at a gas station where the unemployment office was and went straight there.

"Fill out this application," a woman who sat behind a desk told me.

"What for?" I asked.

"You're seeking employment, aren't you?"

"Yes, ma'am."

"We have some minority openings, but you have to fill out an application."

I wasn't sure what she was talking about. I took the pen and paper she handed me to a little desk and sat down and started answering the questions. I write pretty slow, but finally I got to this place where it asked what race I was, and there were six different boxes I could mark. There wasn't one for "half-breed," so after some thought I left them all empty. When I had finished, I took the paper back to the woman.

"Why didn't you mark down your race?" she asked me when she'd read over it.

"I—I wasn't sure of which one, ma'am," I answered. "I'm some of most of it."

"You need to put down your race if you're applying for a minority position."

I still wasn't sure what she was talking about. She wrote something down, and I leaned forward and looked. She had marked me down as a nigger. For a second I got hot, but then remembered my body was a temple and names didn't mean a thing.

I started at the paper mill the next day at minimum wage, working the shift from five in the afternoon till midnight. Rita and the girls slept at the Salvation Army shelter for four nights until I found us a three-room apartment above somebody's garage. The next year was a test of my faith.

That paper mill smelled bad and kept me away from home nights. I missed being under the sun with my feet in the dirt and having a yard and chickens and a vegetable garden.

One night, after I'd been working at the mill six months, a machine broke down and the foreman sent us home early. I walked into our apartment and found Rita sitting facedown at the kitchen table, her head beside a bottle of cheap wine. She looked up surprised, stared at the bottle, then smiled at me.

"Hey, honey. You're home early." She walked over to me and put her arms around my neck.

I kept my hands to my sides. "What are you drinking?"

"Just a little wine. Have a glass with me. Have some."

I remembered finding some empty beer cans on the back steps once, but I had thought the people downstairs threw them there.

"Where are the girls?" I asked.

"In their room. They're asleep. Have some wine, sweetie."

"You know I don't drink, and you're not going to either." I pushed her away and walked to the table.

"Drinking is a sin," I said. I picked up the bottle and tossed it in the trashcan.

"You shouldn't of done that," Rita cried. "It was just a little wine."

"And a little is too much. You're not drinking in my house."

"It's my house too, Elbridge. I stay here all day and night in this tiny place, the girls crying and fussing all the time. The television is broke, and all I got is these walls to stare at. I feel like I'm going crazy."

"Drinking will only make it worse."

Rita put her arms around my neck. "Let's move back to the country. I can't stand this town much longer."

"There's no work in the country right now. I have to stay where there's work."

She put her face next to mine. I could smell the wine on her breath. "Let's not argue. Let's go in the bedroom and be together, honey." She tugged at my arm. "Come on and let's be together."

I pulled away. "You smell like wine. It's a sin to drink."

"It's a sin to be lonely too. I just want you to hold me, honey. Be with me for a while."

"You're drunk." I turned from her and went into the bedroom.

I closed the door and looked at the girls to be sure they were okay, then sat on the edge of the bed and started undressing. Rita was sobbing in the kitchen. I lay back on the mattress and closed my eyes. After a few minutes she stopped crying. Then I heard her searching inside the trashcan.

Lewis

THROUGH THE OPEN BEDROOM WINDOW, Lewis could hear the cooing of mourning doves. Soft light filtered between the curtains and onto the big waterbed where he and Beverly lay. Her head rested on his chest; he stroked her hair and looked down the curves of her breasts and hips. They had made love and Lewis was ready to get up, but he knew he needed to linger a few more minutes.

"I love you, honey," Beverly said.

"Me too," Lewis answered.

"Me too, what?"

"You know."

Beverly sighed. "Lewis, why do you have such a problem saying those words?"

"I just said it."

"You said 'Me too.' The word 'love' is just not part of your vocabulary. I had to make you say it on our wedding night."

"You know I love you. They're just words. I'm laying here beside you, ain't I? I work hard every day and come home at night."

"I know you do. I just wish life hadn't gotten so hectic. We don't talk and do things together nearly as much as we used to." She sighed again. "What do you have planned today?"

"Yard work. I want to look at some land this afternoon, but I thought I'd dig you that flower bed this morning."

Lewis looked between a part in the curtains at a patch of blue sky. "You about ready for some coffee?" he asked.

"In a minute. Wait just a little longer." Beverly rolled onto her stomach. "Let's make a pledge not to argue this week. Let's promise not to argue about a single thing."

"We don't argue more than other people."

"We didn't use to argue at all." She stroked the hair on his chest. "Are you going to join the church tomorrow?"

"I haven't decided."

"It would be good for us. Church would be another part of life we could share."

Lewis stared at the ceiling. Didn't they share breakfast, and then supper every night? Didn't they share Lilly? Hadn't they just done the most sharing thing two people could do?

"I'm still thinking about it."

"Do it, Lewis. Church would be good for us."

Using a shovel and a pickax, Lewis broke up the soil in a four-by-ten-foot plot. He dug out several rocks and stacked them against the backyard fence. The soil, mostly red clay, would have to be mixed with loam and fertilizer. It drained well and was good for supporting houses but was not suited for growing plants. By mid-afternoon, Lewis had framed the plot with treated four-by-fours and shoveled in a hundred pounds of potting soil. In it he set free earthworms bought at the fishing-tackle store, then watched them burrow into the loose dirt. He had created a fertile world where before there was packed clay and rock. A little sweat and some muscle, and a man could do most anything. Why couldn't

Beverly look at what he'd done here and see how much he loved her? Didn't this home and the work he did each week shout how much he cared? Weren't brick and concrete and wood more enduring than words?

Lewis raised his eyes to the sky and saw there was still plenty of sun to go see that piece of land. He collected his tools, washed the dirt off them, and hung them in the garage.

In the kitchen, he swallowed cold tea straight from the pitcher. Beverly, at the counter mixing cake batter, made a face. "Get a glass, Lewis."

"I don't have AIDS."

"You have manners, though."

"I finished your garden."

Beverly put down the mixer and walked over and kissed his chin. "Thank you for the flower bed."

"On the sixth day Lewis created the garden, and he said it was good."

"You shouldn't joke like that."

"Who's joking? Hey, I'm going out to look at that land now. I want you to come with me."

"You want *me* to come to one of your job sites?"

"Yeah. You'll like this place."

Having left Lillian napping with Mabel, the babysitter, Lewis and Beverly drove into the countryside. The trees were streaked with the colors of midautumn: the bright yellow of maples, the crimson and yellow of oaks and hickories, splashes of green from occasional pines and cedars.

"Ain't it beautiful out here?" Lewis said. "You can smell nature." After several miles he turned onto a gravel road that led into the forest.

"Are you sure it's safe here?"

"It's a lot safer than in town. Deer don't carry guns."
About a quarter-mile down the road, Lewis stopped the
car. "Thirty acres of fine virgin forest. We're five miles
from the city limits."

They approached a path that led into the trees. "I
want to show you a rock garden," Lewis said.

"I can't go in there. I'll get my shoes muddy."

"Well, little girl, you're going to have to ride the
horsey." He turned his back to her and squatted. Beverly
laughed, then straddled his back. He rose, his arms
tucked under her legs, and walked into the forest. After
a few yards, he reached his right hand around and
pinched her bottom. She shrieked and slapped him
lightly on the cheek.

"Remember, dear, you're a horsey."

When they came to a creek, Lewis paused before crossing, then stepped from rock to rock. In the middle of
the creek, he lifted one leg and pretended to lose his
balance. Beverly screamed and laughed and grabbed
tighter around his neck. He carried her up the bank and
set her on a large boulder.

"There. Not a speck of dirt on those pretty new
shoes." He sat down beside her. "What do you think of
this place? Nice, ain't it?"

"It's gorgeous. It really is."

"Everything is here. Big trees, rocks. The creek could
be dammed, and a pond flooded. You don't hear any
noise out here. Not a car or siren."

They listened together to the wind in the branches,
the drumming of a woodpecker on a dead tree limb.

"Are you going to build a house out here?" Beverly
asked.

"I might." He clasped her hand. "Bev. What if we

bought this land for ourselves and built out here? Think about it. A big house in the country."

Beverly smiled.

"There are deer all over these woods. I could hunt right over that ridge."

"How could we buy this land, Lewis? You're always saying that we're mortgaged up to our necks."

"I've been thinking about it. We've got a lot of equity in the house. Business is booming. I think maybe we could swing it."

Beverly was still smiling, but her eyes were somber. "You know I'm a city girl."

"The city is only ten minutes away. Hell, the way Chapel Hill is growing, I'm afraid this will be city in ten years."

"Lewis, this is in the country. Lillian wouldn't be able to go to school in Chapel Hill."

"What's the difference?"

"Believe me, I know. There's a big difference."

"We'll put her in private school. Look, I just want you to think about it, okay? Life could be much simpler if we lived out here."

"I'll think about it. Really, I will."

Lewis looked into Beverly's face, then pressed his forehead against hers. "Ever do it on a rock?"

"Nope, and I'm not starting today. There are bugs out here. We have a king-sized waterbed at home."

"Where's that adventurer who used to like doing it beside the river?"

"She's right here, but her back isn't as limber. Turn around, horsey. Take me home."

Lewis smiled sadly as he stooped for Beverly to climb on his back.

*

The next morning, Lewis, Beverly, and Lillian were on their way to church. Beverly attended every Sunday, Lewis accompanying her about once a month. Although he did allow her to tithe his paycheck, the idea of joining the church still bothered him. He hadn't asked many favors from God, and he felt he had received few. Everything he'd accomplished in life, he'd worked hard for. He lived within the law and treated people as they treated him. If anything, he had always been his own man. He made his decisions and lived by them.

Lewis was of the old school when it came to religion: An eye for an eye. If heaven existed, it was some place beyond the clouds where music always played; hell was hotter than fire and terrible. Religion was easier to accept that way—a dreamy collection of stories that he remembered from vacation Bible school, about giants and floods and miracles that you had to believe in with your heart. Believing in something with your heart was simple. Hearts always looked at the good side of life and trusted in love and honesty and peace. Brains didn't work that way. Brains were connected to the eyes and had to look at the real world.

The congregation of Trinity Community Church didn't believe in an eye for an eye. The church was typical Chapel Hill, mostly college-educated whites, with a few blacks and Asians. It operated a soup kitchen and a homeless shelter, it had organized committees against the United States' military involvement in Central America and against apartheid in South Africa, and it had recently gone public in support for gay marriages. The building—a modern rectilinear design in glass and wood, minus steeple and cross—didn't even look to Lewis like a church.

As he walked toward the entrance this morning, Lillian in one arm, Beverly holding the other, several people nodded at him and greeted Beverly.

She pulled at his arm. "Honey, I want you to meet Alice. We're on the fund-raising committee together."

Lewis extended his hand to a slender woman dressed in earth-tone colors. "It's a pleasure to meet you," she told him. "I've heard so much about you. I hope you'll help us next Saturday."

"Oh Lewis, I forgot to tell you," Beverly said. "I was hoping you'd come to the benefit for abused kids and autograph some miniature footballs. We plan to sell them for five dollars each."

"My name ain't worth five dollars. I haven't played ball since college."

"A lot of people remember you," Alice said. "It's all for charity. People will be looking for an excuse to give."

"Can you come, honey?" Beverly asked. "It's in the afternoon."

"I work a lot of Saturdays."

Beverly tightened her grip on his arm and smiled. "Oh, he'll come. He's just being shy."

Charity, Lewis thought. He could have done without the "charity" directed his way when he was a kid. If people pulled their own weight the way he did, there would be no need for charity.

The service began with an interlude of piano and harp, then a quiet minute of reflection. Lewis studied the pastor, or "leader" as she was called here, a middle-aged divorcée with an adopted Korean child. She stood behind the lectern with her eyes closed.

"How many of us would like to be perfect?" the leader began her sermon. "Isn't it the nature of us humans to want to be perfect in everything we do?"

Lewis considered her words. Perfect? No, he didn't want to be perfect. A football game with everyone playing perfectly? No one would win. Life was set up for winners and losers. Hunting would be no challenge if a man never missed a shot. If the world were perfect, then Lewis would never have been hungry, and hunger and need had gotten him all he possessed now.

"God doesn't expect us to be perfect," the leader said. "That's what salvation is all about. Forgiveness. God doesn't expect us to do everything just right because It knows we are mortal. It just wants us to ask forgiveness when we have sinned."

When did God become an "it"? Lewis wondered.

"God is perfect, and only perfection can be tolerant of imperfection. We are humans and have difficulty understanding our faults and the faults of others, but God can understand and forgive. We are not God, and we are not expected to be perfect."

Lewis began to like what the leader was saying. Maybe God was similar to a referee, who knew all the rules and was there to enforce them if necessary, but who mostly just watched the game being played. Humans were the players—they could bend the rules a little, as long as they played hard and didn't mess up the flow of the game and God didn't throw down the flag. Maybe God respected you even more when you played to win.

"It is when we realize we are imperfect that we are forgiven," the leader said. "God doesn't expect us to be perfect but he does expect us to ask forgiveness."

The leader paused and lowered her face as the organ music began. "If anyone seeks forgiveness, may he or she come forward and say so in front of the church and God. Only when we confess our weaknesses are we pure and clean."

Lewis watched a few people come forward and whisper in the leader's ear, then return to their seats. Beverly placed her hand on his leg. Lewis took a deep breath. At the least, joining the church made good business sense: nearly all his colleagues belonged to some church, and he knew how much Beverly wanted him to join. Lewis stepped to the aisle and walked forward.

"I'd like to join the church," he said to the pastor.

She smiled and grasped his hands. "Do you ask forgiveness for your imperfections?"

"I do."

"Do you wish to be baptized and to receive Holy Communion?"

"Yes."

"What is your name?"

"Lewis Calhoon."

"Praise God," the pastor said loudly. "May I present to the church our new brother, Lewis, who stands before us this morning a perfect man."

Together with a young woman who also had come forward this morning, Lewis was led to a room in the rear of the church to wait while the altar was prepared for Baptism. He stared through an open window at the bright day outside, then looked at the young woman. She was pretty, and her white skirt showed the curves of her body. He averted his gaze, suddenly remembering where he was and why he was there, and stared again out the window. A mockingbird sang loudly from the branches of a gum tree, mimicking the notes of every bird in the churchyard. In his mind, Lewis saw Mrs. Bullard marching to the front of the church and whispering in the preacher's ear, to be washed sinless and guilt-free.

It ain't that easy, Lewis thought. You're supposed to

feel something, and I don't. I've never been a hypocrite, and I shouldn't start now. I play by the rules, and the rules are what matter.

Lewis opened the back door of the room. The breeze washed his face; he smelled the rich musk of autumn. The clear sky arched above him like the dome of a great cathedral. Me and you understand each other just fine, he thought as he gazed upward. Let's leave it at that.

He went back inside and found Beverly in the sanctuary. "I'm not ready for this yet," he whispered to her. "I'll wait in the car."

Faces turned as he strode down the aisle and through the swinging front doors.

Beverly was silent during lunch; hurt filled her eyes. Immediately after eating, she went to her bedroom.

Lewis drank a few beers while watching a football game, then, when he had put Lillian down for her nap, went to the bedroom, where Beverly lay on the bed, her face in the pillow. He sat beside her.

"Hey, look, I'm sorry. It just wasn't right for me."

Beverly didn't speak for several seconds. "You embarrassed me."

"Well, don't you think I was a little embarrassed marching up there in front of all those people?"

"I was proud of you."

"Proud of me acting like I'm weak?"

Beverly rolled over and looked at Lewis. Her eyes were shiny. "What are you so afraid of? Why can't you ask for help once in a while?"

"I don't need any help."

"You do. More than you realize. You're always the

warrior, the tough guy, battling the world. Can't you be more of a family man?"

"My God, ain't we a family. I'm home every night."

"We don't talk anymore. It's you and your work and hunting, and when you come home, it's supper and bed. And you start all over again the next morning."

"It takes a lot to keep a construction company going. You spend enough time with your committees."

"That's because you're always gone. I want us to do things together. Church would be something we could share."

"I'll go to church. I just don't need to be another of those hypocrites."

Beverly's eyes flashed with anger. "Do you think I'm a hypocrite?"

"No. Just some of those people."

"Today when Alice asked you to sign autographs, couldn't you just have said yes?"

"Look, Bev, I don't know the first thing about fund-raising. Besides, it's not my business to go sticking my nose in other people's lives. I don't abuse Lilly, and I don't expect other people to abuse their children. I live my life the best I can, and I expect others to do the same."

"There's all kinds of abuse, Lewis."

"What do you mean?"

Beverly sat up. "I don't think I've ever heard you tell Lillian that you love her. You hold her and play with her, but you never say those words."

Lewis's face flushed. "You know damn well I love her more than anything."

"Then just say it sometimes. I have to force you to ever say it to me."

"Words are just what they are—wind."

"You smell like beer."

"Well, it's Sunday afternoon. I was watching the game."

"You didn't use to drink so much beer. I smell it on you almost every night when you come home."

"A few beers don't hurt anything. Look, I'm a good father and husband, and you have no right to accuse me of anything different."

Beverly grasped his hand. "I know you are, Lewis. You are. But you're more and more caught up in your work, and there's a wall growing between us. Sometimes I feel we're just playing marriage now, not living it the way we used to."

"I try hard, Bev. The day I saw Lilly in the delivery room, I swore that she was never going to do without. I have a crew depending on me, and it takes a lot of time and work. I hit the floor running every day."

"I know you do, and you need to slow down." Beverly paused and wiped away a tear. She looked into his eyes. "Maybe we need to have some counseling. I know plenty of people who were really helped by counseling."

"This whole damn town is in counseling. I'm not going to no shrink."

"Think about it, honey. I want us to talk and share our problems. I don't want us living in separate worlds."

Lewis heard Lilly crying in her bedroom. He sighed and squeezed his wife's hand, and went for his child.

During the next week, Lewis and his men finished the rafters on the house at the development, leaving it to the roofers to hammer on cedar shingles, and to the electricians to wire the place before the Sheetrock was put in. Lewis juggled the schedules of the different contracted crews, and made telephone calls to order materials and check about permits. Pete and his coworkers moved to another site where the foundation had been laid and began framing again. On Friday afternoon, after paying his crew, Lewis went to his office to schedule the next week's work. He was drinking his second beer when Rachel knocked on his door and came in.

"You can go," he said without looking up. "I'm going to be here awhile."

"It's five-thirty, Lewis."

He nodded and kept writing. Rachel remained in the doorway. "You work too much," she told him.

Exhaling heavily, he pushed back his chair and looked at her. "I have to."

"Are you going hunting again tomorrow morning? Is it still hunting season?"

"Yeah. And boy, am I looking forward to it."

Rachel wet her lips with her tongue. "Ah, Allen's leaving tonight for a convention in Charlotte. Why don't you drop by the house tomorrow morning after you get through hunting and I'll cook you breakfast." She stared into Lewis's eyes.

"I don't eat much breakfast."

"We'll have coffee. Talk some. It would be nice."

"Yeah, well, maybe I will. I mean, if I get out of the woods in time." Lewis clasped his hands behind his head. "Nothing wrong with having a little coffee."

Rachel smiled. "I'll expect you. I make great omelets." Without another word, she turned and left.

Lewis arrived home at a few minutes before eight. Beverly was hosting the weekly Junior League meeting. He quickly kissed her on the cheek and greeted the other women in the living room before going to see Lillian, who was with Mabel in her room. He found supper in the oven, and ate it with the latest *Sports Illustrated* as company. Then he went out the back door and sat on the steps. A large moon was rising in the east—a hunter's moon, its crisp white light bathing the tree branches. Lewis thought of all the work he had scheduled for the coming week, and tried to recall when he had last had the time to watch the moon come up.

It occurred to him that he'd left his clipboard in the truck, and he walked around the side of the house to retrieve it. At the partly open living room window, he stopped when he heard his name. He saw that the women still at the meeting were all leaning forward and smiling.

"He's too big to beat up," Beverly was saying. She laughed. "Sometimes I want to knock him over the head with a club and tell him to wake up. Work and sleep, that's all he ever does anymore. Except for hunting. He'll get out of bed an hour before sunrise to go sit in a tree and try to shoot a deer."

Claudia sipped from her cup, then dabbed her painted lips with a napkin. "You *really* have my sympathy," she said. "He sounds like a real beast."

"Yes," Debra chimed in. "I am *so* sorry for you."

Beverly blinked and frowned. "What's that tone of voice all about?"

"Where is Lewis right now?" Claudia asked. "Out at a bar?"

"No," Beverly answered. "He's finishing his supper."

"Well," Claudia said. "Right now my husband is sitting on a stool in the Carolina Coffee Shop, tippling his fifth or sixth martini with his lawyer buddies. He'll stagger in about midnight, smelling like gin. He'll wake me up and say he wants to make love, then ask me to blow him. *Real* romantic."

"Yeah," Debra agreed. "I could tell the same story. But at least you *have* a husband. It'll be a year next month since Mike left me for that little bitch in one of his classes. He's living with her while demanding that we sell the house so he can have his half of the money. You really have it tough, Beverly."

"Okay." Beverly twisted her napkin. "I admit Lewis has his good qualities. But he won't talk to me. Not *really* talk, as we do."

"Pity, pity." Claudia placed her hand over her heart.

"Really, Beverly, does he have to talk?" Debra said. "Can't you be content to just sit and look at him? I mean, the man is a hunk."

"Drool over him is what I'd do," Claudia said. "I'd tell him to shut up and take his clothes off."

"Yes!" Debra leaned low over the table. "Tell us— how is he in bed? Give us the dirty details."

Beverly blushed crimson. "Y'all are terrible!" She tossed her head back. "Maybe I don't have it so bad. But it could be even better. I want us to get some counseling, and he won't even discuss it."

"Oh, it might could be better," Debra said. "But believe me, it could be a whole lot worse."

Lewis smiled at the conversation, flattered that a woman would still call him a hunk. He felt more like a mule these days, a beast of burden with too much work heaped on his back.

Clipboard in hand, he entered the house through the back door. He and Mabel talked for a few minutes before she went home, and he was left to put Lillian into her pajamas. He sat in a large rocking chair with her on his lap and read to her from *The Cat in the Hat* until her eyes began to blink, then close, and her head drooped against him. He kissed her forehead; she smelled sweetly of baby powder. After putting her into her bed and tucking the covers under her chin, he went to the small extra bedroom he used as an office. There he sat at his desk and unrolled the blueprint of the latest house under construction. The wall clock had chimed ten when Beverly walked in and placed her hands on his shoulders.

"I thought Debra and Claudia would never leave," she said. "I am talked to death."

"How'd it go?"

"Oh, fine."

Lewis felt Beverly trace her fingertips across his chin as if studying the texture of his skin. He needed a shave, and the cleft in his chin had deepened with the weight he'd gained since his football days. She moved her fingers to his cheekbones. "You're getting crow's-feet, Lewis." She massaged the corners of his eyes.

"I'm getting old."

Beverly kissed the top of his head. "You're not over the hill yet. You got a compliment tonight."

"I did? What?"

"Why don't you put your work away and come on to bed, and I'll tell you."

"I need about ten more minutes."

Beverly moved her hands to his shoulders and kneaded the tight muscles beneath his shirt. "I was talking with Debra tonight about babies. You and I haven't talked about another baby for a while. I'm not getting any younger."

Lewis looked up. The light from the desk lamp lit his wife's face like the full moon outside the window.

Elbridge

THE BIRDS WERE FLYING. The sun was below the treeline, and the air was cold and sharp. A light frost coated the stubble of cut corn. I was sitting on an empty lard bucket, following the flights of doves as they swooped over. My watch said five minutes to seven, and I was about busting to shoot. I had the whole side of the field to myself. Across it, I could see some men; three weeks had passed since opening day, and all the one-time hunters were home in bed.

I sat with my back to a hedge, wearing a camo hat so that orangey hair of mine wouldn't stand out. I looked at my watch; only three minutes left. I chambered a shell and dipped my head.

"Lord, please bless my eye today and let me get some birds. I'll eat every one of them. Amen."

Suddenly a volley of shots rang out from the other side of the field. I looked at my watch—I'd set it by the car radio driving over—and knew someone was breaking the law. More shots rang out. One person jumps the gun, everybody does. I kept my eyes on the second hand till it hit the twelve.

Five doves were coming toward me over the treeline. I clicked off the safety and stood and swung up my gun, sighted on the lead bird, fired, jacked in another shell and shot again. Two doves fell. I marked the spot in the field. Already another flight was coming in from across the field, and the men over there were shooting. The birds were dipping and flying stutter-wing; three of them fell, one winged his way through. I waited and sighted on him, led him and knocked him down. The sky was clear now, so I clicked on the safety and walked out to get my birds.

The doves flew thick for a half-hour after the sun rose. Between flights, I ate a can of Viennas and drank a Pepsi. A group of birds came in from my left, and the lead bird saw me and fluttered and tried to turn, but I pumped out three shots and got three doves. I had that feeling now where I was part of something bigger than me, and I let the spirit fill me and guide my eye.

Fourteen doves lay in a pile at my feet when the sun had cleared the treetops. Fifteen was the limit, and I wanted another shot. But like a whistle had sounded, the doves had quit flying, and they probably wouldn't be up much again until midafternoon. I unchambered my shells and put them in my pocket, then stuffed the birds into an old onion sack.

I started across the field toward my car. The other hunters were coming in too. They had a springer spaniel with them. I was about fifty yards away, when one of them threw his gun up and started shooting. A single dove was flying over them. The other men started shooting, but that dove kept dodging and darting. I pulled a shell from my pocket and chambered it.

The dove got through all that shooting and was coming at me. I sighted in with my gun. Somebody was still shooting, but I knew the dove was out of his range. I led the bird and knocked him down. He landed a few yards from my feet.

"That's my bird," one of the hunters shouted. They

were walking over, the dog running in circles with his nose to the ground.

"That's my bird," the man repeated when he was close.

"I think I got him, fellows," I said. "I think he was past . . ."

"No. Hell, no. I saw feathers fly on my last shot."

I bent and picked up the bird. There was blood on his frontside. "Sir, you were shooting behind the bird. He was coming right at me. See the blood on his breast?"

"Bullshit, buddy. I ain't losing that bird."

"He hit it," another man said. "I saw the feathers."

They were all white men and older than me. I didn't know 'em. "Well, I . . ."

"Well hell! Toss me my bird."

I felt the blood pounding in my ears. If there had been just one man, I would've fought. I tossed the dove on the ground, and the dog took it in his mouth. Then I started walking off.

One of the men chuckled. "The little mongrel fucker," I heard him say.

I slowed down my old Chrysler and turned onto the bumpy road that snaked through the trailer park. I wasn't mad any longer and kinda pitied that man who'd taken my bird. He and his buddies could call me names, but I knew on the inside I was pure. Besides, I had fourteen doves and a whole lot more to be thankful for.

For a year I had stayed on second shift. Many a night when I came home I could smell wine or beer on Rita's breath. But I kept praying and talking to her. I knew her drinking was a test of my faith. Then, all inside a week, I got a pay raise and got moved to first shift. We moved into a trailer that was twice the size of the garage apartment. It wasn't fancy, but it had a yard. Two months later, Rita found out she was pregnant. She didn't drink a drop after that. I knew this one was going to be a boy. I was going to name him Nathan, after my grandpa.

As I pulled up, I could see blue flashes through the window, and knew the girls were watching cartoons. I took the birds over to a spigot beside the garbage can and started cleaning them. My grandpa had shown me how to dress birds by pulling out the breast, then stripping off the skin and feathers and washing off the blood. In ten minutes, I had a paper plate full of fresh purple meat. Like manna dropped from heaven.

One of the Mexican kids who lived next door was watching me from beside his trailer. I wondered if I might ought to share some of the meat with his family, but I reasoned from all the beans and chili I had seen his kind eat in the fields that they probably wouldn't be fond of dove meat. I waved at the kid, and he ducked around the corner.

The girls were still glued to the television when I walked in. Rita sat at the kitchen table, staring into her coffee. Smoke curled from the cigarette she held.

"Look what Pop has," I said to the girls.

Cindy wrinkled her nose. "Yuuuck!" She looked back at the television. Rita glanced up from the table as I carried the meat to the sink.

"Good morning, sweetheart. I love you." I dipped to kiss her forehead.

She pulled away and hugged herself. "Get those away from me, Elbridge."

"They were flying today. I got fourteen. Well, really fifteen." I put the plate in the sink and looked at Rita.

Even with the thirty pounds she had gained since I married her, she still had a pretty face. She hadn't begun to show yet, but her breasts were swollen. "Did you sleep okay last night?"

"I woke up when you started the car."

"I tried to be quiet. It's that busted muffler."

"I was sick again." She forced a smile. "You got a lot of birds, honey?"

"The limit. They were flying pretty."

Rita nodded. "Will you pour me some more coffee?" She held out her cup.

I hesitated before taking it, then lifted the percolator, which felt half empty. She struck a match for a cigarette. Babies and cigarettes aren't a good mix, but I wasn't gonna fuss at her. At least she had stopped drinking. I poured coffee in her cup halfway, filled the rest with milk, and put the cup under her face. She was looking down again. I went and picked Connie up, hugged her, and tickled her stomach. She squirmed and laughed, her eyes fastened on Bugs Bunny all the time. I rubbed her head and set her back on the couch. "I love you two buggers," I said. Cindy and Connie didn't answer.

"I'm going to wash up," I yelled out. The floor of the old trailer creaked, the bathroom door was off its roller, but this didn't bother me. I was feeling good. Hunting always did that to me: standing under that big sky, the shotgun sounding like thunder, the birds falling like rain from above. I was the farmer who went to the field and collected the harvest. Looking into them clouds, I became a part of something big and strong, and all I had to do was believe and look and point and pull the trigger and jack in another shell, and not think, but act on faith. The Bible said a man could do anything if he had enough faith—move a mountain or knock his supper down from the sky.

In the mirror, I looked on past my reflection with eyes of faith, and saw a little house in the country with a garden, and shade trees in the yard. The girls were playing under the tree. Best of all, there were diapers hanging on the clothesline to dry, and inside that house was my newborn son, and he was a beautiful child.

Lewis

LEWIS DRESSED QUIETLY in the dark, pulling on long underwear, then jeans and a flannel shirt, thick wool socks, insulated camo jumpsuit, and finally his boots. Outside, the streetlights still shone brightly; dawn was two hours away.

Nestled under the covers, Beverly slept serenely. Lillian had awakened during the night and climbed into the bed, and she too slept soundly now. Lewis stood over his wife and child and paused. He placed his hand on the curve of Beverly's hip.

I do love you. I might not say it, but I do.

Lillian slept with her rump in the air, the blanket down around her feet. Lewis straightened his daughter and pulled the blanket up. When he stroked her hair, she mumbled in her sleep. I'm one lucky fucker, he thought. He felt guilt at not having immediately refused Rachel's invitation to breakfast; he was ashamed that the idea appealed to him and that a dozen times he had thought about stopping by her house. "I'll be back soon," he whispered.

For Lewis in his tree stand beside the river, the physical world existed in the mind alone. He sat erect, his eyes closed, in woods as silent as they were dark. He could not feel the boundaries of his body, and he wondered if this was what death was like—silence and darkness, mind suspended by itself in the recesses of the universe, awaiting whatever happened to the soul.

Lewis welcomed the peace. Here he had only himself to answer to, only his own needs to meet, no explanations or excuses to give anyone. The hours here were a time-out, during which regular rules and demands were lifted, and he was able to rest.

He opened his eyes. In the sky to the east, Venus shone brilliant; dawn was arriving as a faint pink curtain. The forest floor was still black, but Lewis knew from rubs and tracks that somewhere in a thicket nearby was a big buck, lying in a hollow he had stomped with his hooves. Just the buck and a couple of favored does. Lewis judged that the buck was awake now and was seeing that faint glow of the coming day, that he would remain in the warmth of his bed but within the hour would rise and come to the river to drink. Now was the waiting time, when seconds stretched.

The pink dawn turned scarlet and gradually swallowed Venus. Lewis could make out contrasts in the darkness below him, tree trunks against the ground cover, the edge where earth met water. The river gathered light from the sky and reflected the morning's glow. Upriver, a beaver smacked its tail. A songbird warbled, and mallards quacked from a reed thicket.

When he heard a twig snap, Lewis felt a surge of adrenaline. He gripped his rifle and stared at the sandbar beside the river, then brought his weapon off his lap and raised it. He kept his thumb on the safety.

The brace of mallards beat their wings against the surface of the water and took to the air. Lewis watched their flight. When he turned his eyes back to the river-bank, he was jolted. A doe stood clear on the sand, a ghost that had drifted in. She sniffed the sand, took a couple of steps, sniffed again. She signaled with a flip of her tail, and two fawns joined her.

Now the big buck arrived. Lewis watched him emerge: black muzzle, eyes and ears, head sporting a huge rack. Lewis had never seen such antlers: at least ten points, and curved like a pair of wings. The buck slipped into the clearing, swinging his head from side to side, his nostrils heaving. He continued his slow steps until his neck was visible, then his shoulders, bunched with muscles. Lewis brought his rifle up slowly and centered the crosshairs in the scope on a spot behind the animal's front legs. He exhaled, a long breath, and squeezed off the round.

The rifle kicked into his shoulder, and the rest of the world disappeared. Time stopped, and in the shattered seconds, the buck flinched, then turned his head toward the sound. He seemed to be looking directly at the tree, but his eyes had gone dim as life passed from him. His front legs buckled, and he sank headfirst into the sand; the forest behind him was ripped apart by the flight of his herd. Lewis clicked on the safety and lowered the weapon, as the buck rolled on his side.

Lewis sat for a few minutes and let his breath and heartbeat slow. The forest was now silent again, and when he felt the buck was dead, Lewis left the tree stand.

A heart shot—the buck had died instantly—Lewis found when he reached the animal. And the deer was even bigger than he had estimated from the rubs and tracks. Twelve points. He had seen such racks only in photographs.

"I thank you, old man," he whispered. "You lived long and good, and you died quick, and that is all I could ask for."

Lewis slipped his gutting knife from its sheath. He field-dressed the deer, and dumped the lungs, guts, and stomach in the river. He pierced the thick cartilage between the animal's nostrils, then took a length of rope from one pocket, threaded it through the hole, and began dragging the deer to his truck.

As the city limits drew closer, Lewis tried to block out the little voice in his mind. *God, she's pretty, and so damn feminine. I could stop and just have some coffee and talk a little. I don't think she was really coming on to me. Wouldn't be nothing wrong with having some coffee. I love how she laughs. Sexy as hell.*

Approaching the turn that led to Rachel's house, Lewis felt his abdominal muscles grow taut. He gripped the steering wheel hard, remembering the picture of Beverly and Lillian earlier that morning, and the love he had felt for them. At the intersection, he drove straight through, without even looking toward Rachel's. A joy inside his chest grew with each heartbeat: the treasure he had could not be traded away. He thought of Lilly's tranquil face, where the union of his and Beverly's spirit and body and love was reflected. What loss he had carried from his own boyhood was regained there, in his child. The gulf that had grown between him and Beverly could be bridged, the wounds healed before they festered. If she wanted him to join the church, he'd do it. The act didn't mean anything, it would take nothing from him. He'd join the coming Sunday. He and Beverly needed some time away; he'd take her back to Disney World—no, one of those cruises in the Caribbean. They'd get pregnant again. When his son was twelve, he'd give him a rifle as his own father had done, but when the boy climbed into that tree stand for the first time, Lewis would be with him.

Several trucks were parked at Johnny's Hook and Bullet when Lewis arrived. Besides Pete, he saw Bill Lambert, a plumber he sometimes contracted, standing with some other hunters at his tailgate. Lewis stepped from his truck and adjusted the canvas covering his deer, then walked over to the group.

"Boss man," Pete greeted him. "Ain't you gonna show us what you got back there?"

"Howdy, fellows," Lewis said. He saw the eight-point buck lying in the bed of Bill's pickup. "You got a nice one there."

"Biggest one killed this year." Bill laughed. "I got you fellows beat."

Lewis smiled. He had had some arguments with Bill in the past over shoddy work and failure to meet deadlines. "Yeah, you got a real nice kill," he said.

Pete studied Lewis's face. His eyes darted toward Lewis's truck. "I wouldn't be too damn fast to claim victory. You ain't seen what Lewis has under that canvas."

Bill pursed his lips. "What you got, Lewis?"

"Just a deer."

"You ashamed to show it?"

"Shit," Pete said. "I'll bet you a twenty on the spot that the boss man has killed a bigger deer. Twenty bucks, Bill."

Bill looked at Lewis, then back to his eight-pointer. "I'll take your twenty," he told Pete. "Show us what you got, Lewis."

Lewis's buck weighed in at a hundred seventy pounds gutted. The rack, twenty-two inches between the inside curves, with a five-and-a-half-inch base, claimed an unofficial county record. Word spread among the hunters converging from the field, and soon they were gathering around Lewis.

"God damn," Pete said, smiling broadly. He wore a twenty-dollar bill in the cuff of his hat. "This boy could shit gold turds."

Bill brought a fifth of George Dickel from his truck. He opened the full bottle and turned it up, then held it toward Lewis. "It's on me, man. That's a hell of a deer."

Lewis stared at the bottle. He hadn't had a drink of whiskey since college. "No thanks, Bill. You keep it."

"Hell, buddy, have you gotten too good to drink with me? I know this ain't Wild Turkey, but I'm no big-time contractor either." Bill smiled, but his eyes were cold.

Silence fell over the hunters. "Hit it, boss man," Pete finally said. "You just got more famous."

One drink wouldn't hurt, Lewis thought. One drink was like one beer. He took the bottle and tipped it. The whiskey burned going down. Pete thrust a beer chaser at him, and Lewis took a long swallow.

Bill nodded at the hunters, then walked to his truck. He spun his tires leaving.

"Hot damn, you took his lunch," Pete said.

"I wasn't trying to make him mad."

"You bested his deer, I took his twenty, and he left you a bottle of whiskey. What a morning."

"What'd you kill that deer with?" one of the hunters asked.

"Browning two-seventy stainless." Lewis opened his cab and pulled the rifle from behind the seat. "This little baby."

A chorus of whistles went off. Lewis felt a pleasant buzz spreading across his forehead. He had forgotten what good whiskey felt like when it hit the bloodstream. He drank again from the bottle, then finished off the beer. Somebody handed him another cold one.

"Can I hold it?" asked Frank, a college kid who worked for Lewis part-time. Lewis gave him the rifle, and the boy's eyes gleamed as he slid the bolt up, back, and forward. The smooth oiled metal moved soundlessly while he chambered a round.

"The law's here," someone announced.

Lewis turned and saw a jeep with state tags pulling into the parking lot. A uniformed game warden got out. "Heard somebody got a real horse," the warden said. "Johnny called me. I just need to see the hunter a minute."

"Frank, put my rifle in the rack," Lewis said. He stepped forward and shook the warden's hand.

"You're the lucky one?" the warden asked. "Where do I know you from?"

"Before he started slaying moose," Pete interrupted, "he used to slay quarterbacks."

"Yeah. I remember now. I remember seeing you play. How about stepping over here and let me check your license and see that the deer's tagged." Lewis and Pete followed the warden to the scale. The warden measured the rack, then congratulated Lewis and left. The bourbon came out again, and Lewis took two more slugs before waving the bottle away.

He was on a cloud as he drove home. With his stomach empty and his heart pumping hard with excitement, the alcohol had gone straight to his head. The day seemed unusually bright, and his thoughts and plans of the morning were illuminated by the whiskey.

I'll tell her to start packing as soon as I get home, Lewis thought. We'll take a week's cruise and screw all day long. I'll join the church, and we'll stop arguing over little things. Lilly ain't going to grow up like me. We're going to have a son, and I'll take him hunting and fishing and teach him to play ball.

On impulse, while driving beside the development where he was working, Lewis braked and turned into the entrance. He'd check to see that the crew had secured all equipment; a couple of months back he'd lost a miter saw and fifty pounds of nails to thieves.

The latest house, finished except for trim work, smelled of new wood and paint. Lewis walked through the rooms admiring the details. Within a month a family would be moving in. With these studs, beams, and boards, Lewis and his crew had created the center of somebody's world. One day, not before too long, he would direct the construction of a new home for himself and Beverly and the babies.

Lewis stopped in his tracks—sticking through the doorway of the utility room was a man's leg, in gray trousers and a dirty, laceless sneaker. Lewis recognized the clothes of the homeless man he had fired. Anger flushed his cheeks: the bum was trashing up his new house, probably sleeping off a drunk. Lewis went to the doorway and looked inside the small room.

The man was wrapped in a tattered blanket. Beside him on the floor was an empty pint bottle of wine and a half-eaten can of Vienna sausages. His face was hidden by the blanket.

"Hey, buddy," Lewis said. The man didn't move. "Hey, wake up." He tapped the man's leg with the toe of his boot, then leaned over cautiously and pulled down the blanket. Hair was matted to his skull, and a string of saliva had leaked from his lips to the floor; his skin was the color of clay. He was stone dead.

"God almighty," Lewis said. He stepped backward, nauseated by the sight and smell of the huddled form.

He went directly to his truck, and began to call 911 on his cellular phone, then paused and clicked off the receiver. An ambulance roaring up here with flashing lights? The paper might pick it up. Who would want a brand-new house that already harbored a homeless ghost? He would call Pete instead, hoping he'd be home by now.

"Yo?"

"Hey, Pete, it's Lewis. I need you to come over to the house on Summerwood."

"What's wrong? We been robbed again?"

"No. Something worse. Come on over, and I'll show you."

"Froze to death," Pete said later as he looked at the corpse. "It got down in the twenties last night. He drank his wine and passed out and froze dead." Pete pulled a fifth of bourbon from his coat pocket. "You look like you need a shot of this."

Lewis took a long swallow. "I wish to hell he'd picked another place to freeze. It won't help sell this place."

"Boss man, I can see the newspaper headline: 'Homeless man freezes after being fired by wealthy contractor.' " Pete chuckled.

"It's not funny." Lewis bubbled the whiskey again. "I was thinking of taking some vacation time."

Pete lifted the edge of the blanket and covered the man's face. He chewed his lip. "Look, our friend here just happened to freeze on your property. They probably ran him out of the shelter for being drunk. What if I move him to a more proper place for a drunk to freeze?"

"What do you mean?"

"We didn't kill him. I don't think there's a law against moving a person that died of natural causes. I could wait till dark and move him behind a dumpster in town. Jimmy would help me."

"I'll pay you each a hundred dollars," Lewis said in a rush.

"At your service." Pete held out his hand. Lewis counted out ten twenty-dollar bills from his wallet.

Lewis took several deep breaths at the front door. He wished he hadn't had those last shots of whiskey, and wondered how what had started out as such a fine day could have soured so terribly. Rifle in hand, he opened the door and entered the living room.

"Hello, dear," Beverly called from the kitchen. "That you?"

"Yeah."

Lewis leaned his rifle against the wall. He was drunker

than he had been in years. He closed his eyes to stop his head from spinning. When he opened them, Beverly was walking into the living room.

"Any luck?" she asked. Her face was clean of makeup, her hair gathered into a ponytail. She wore old faded blue jeans and a T-shirt, her nipples pressing against the thin fabric.

"God, Bev," he said. "You look like you're back in college."

"I have a surprise for you." She pointed to the couch, where a suitcase had been packed. "I made us reservations at the beach."

"Wait. I've got one for you first. We going to go . . ."

Lewis wobbled backward. He touched the wall to steady himself.

"Are you all right, honey?" Beverly asked.

"Yeah, yeah. I'm all right." He closed his eyes for a few seconds. "I need to sit down. I had a little too much whiskey."

Beverly's forehead creased with worry lines. "Lewis, you never drink whiskey. And in the morning?"

"Yeah, I know. I shot a big deer, but I have something more important to tell you. Let me put my rifle up. I want to tell you my surprise."

The whiskey had taken Lewis's balance, and as he reached for the gun, the toe of his boot hit the stock and made it fall. He lunged for the rifle, but missed, and the weapon smacked barrel-first against the arm of the oak rocking chair.

The chambered round burst from the gun, punched through the middle of Beverly's chest, and buried itself in the wall. Beverly's eyes opened wide, and her mouth formed an O, as if in that millisecond she saw something awesome; she raised her arms into the air. Lewis caught her as she fell forward. He lifted his wife over one shoulder, then ran screaming into the yard.

Elbridge

I WAS WHISTLING as I drove back home. I'd found a muffler at a junkyard that cost about a third what a new one did. At the Mini Mart, I stopped and bought a jug of Pepsi and some charcoal. I was feeling good from the hunt that morning, and figured I'd splurge and grill the dove breasts.

The girls were still froze in front of the television when I walked in the trailer. "Y'all need to cut that thing off and get outside and play," I said. "That TV will ruin your brain."

"Hey, Rita," I called, "we're gonna grill out."

Nothing came back but the voices of the Muppet Babies. I went to the rear of the trailer, but it was empty.

"Cindy. Where's your mother?" I asked.

"She left."

I turned her face toward me and leaned down to her. "Left for where?"

"She said she was going to the store."

"When did she go?"

"Right after you left."

"How'd she go?"

"She walked."

The pit of my stomach went cold. I went to the refrigerator and saw that we had plenty of milk and coffee. Maybe she was out of cigarettes. Rita would walk ten miles if she ran out of smokes.

"Please, God," I prayed. "Don't let her fall again."

The girls were hungry, so I made them bologna sandwiches. I went outside and cleaned the grill, then put the muffler on the car. Two hours passed, and still no sign of Rita. I started the charcoal.

"When's Mommy coming home?" Cindy whined from where she and Connie were playing house in a big cardboard box.

"Mommy loves you. She'll be here soon."

I cooked the dove meat and made some rice, then heated up a can of green beans, and me and the girls went ahead and ate. Darkness was settling, and I wondered why the day had started so good and then had to end this way. Then I remembered that God had a reason for everything He does, and that man is not to question His acts.

At about nine that night, a car stopped in front of the trailer. The girls ran to the door and opened it. Rita stood there rocking on her feet. Beyond her, I saw a car pulling away that looked loaded down. Rita lurched up the steps and headed straight for the couch, without even looking at me.

"You sick again, Mommy?" Connie asked, her little face worried.

"I'm okay, baby." She fumbled to light a cigarette.

She needed food in her. I filled a glass with milk and put two dove breasts on a plate. "Eat this, Rita. You need to eat."

Her eyes were flat, glassy. "I ain't hungry."

"Eat," I told her. "You'll be sick if you don't eat."

She stared dumbly at the pieces of meat, then picked one up and threw it across the room. "Fly away, birdie." She cackled and threw the other breast. "Fly away, birdie. I wish the hell *I* could." She looked at me through the cigarette smoke.

"You girls go to your room," I said. "Mommy ain't feeling real good. Go on now." They kissed their mother's cheek, then left with large, sad eyes.

"Drink this milk," I said.

"I don't want any milk."

"You need to drink it. You need to drink it for the baby."

"I don't need no damn milk, and I don't want another damn baby." Rita searched in her purse and pulled out a pint bottle of wine. She looked me in the eyes as she unscrewed the cap and took a swallow.

"Why are you doing this to us?" I was taking deep breaths to keep down my anger.

" 'Cause I want to. 'Cause this trailer stinks, and we don't have any money, and I'm having another baby." She took another drink. " 'Cause you're so high and mighty and perfect, and you expect me to be the same."

When she started to raise the bottle again, my anger boiled over and I grabbed her arm. "You're not drinking in here. You ain't killing that baby." I twisted the bottle from her hand and went to the sink.

"Don't pour that out," she shouted. "That's all I got." She held my arm, then raked her nails down the side of my face. I dropped the bottle and whirled around and gripped her shoulder to stop her. The top button of her blouse popped open, and at the base of her neck I saw two purple hickeys. Rage hit me like a hammer.

"Who did this?" I hollered. "Who you been with?"

Rita's mouth curled in a sneer. "What does it matter? At least he had some money."

"You whore!"

She slapped me. Over her shoulder, I could see the girls. Cindy was crying.

"I hate you," Rita shouted. "I hate your damn preaching to me, and I hate your dead-ass God, and . . ."

My fist came up before I could stop it, and smashed into her jaw. Rita reeled backward. She put her hand to her lips, where a trickle of blood had started, and spit on the floor. Both the babies were screaming. That was the first time I'd ever hit her.

"Rita, I—I'm sorry," I said. "I didn't mean to."

She staggered across the room and grabbed her purse, then pushed the girls with her into their bedroom. I heard her slide the bolt latch shut from inside. As I stood by the door, I could hear the bedsprings squeaking, and the girls crying. "Open up, Rita. I didn't mean to hit you."

"Get the hell away from me."

I choked back a sob and went into our bedroom, and fell facedown across the mattress. The tears came as all this rage and shame poured from me. Then I fell asleep.

I dreamed of eggs frying. The grease was too hot, and heat and smoke were rolling up from the pan into my eyes. I was trying to lift the eggs with a spatula, but they tore apart and started burning.

When I woke up, I remembered Rita and the hickeys and me hitting her. I still smelled the eggs burning and felt the heat from the grease. I opened my eyes wider and saw the room was filled with smoke. I jumped up and ran to the girls' bedroom, where I could see light flickering under the door.

"Rita!" I screamed. The door handle was so hot it

burned my palm. I pounded on the wood: it was warm. I rammed the door with my shoulder, and finally it cracked and splintered, and burst outward in a big ball of flame. I sucked in fire and felt it burn all the way into my lungs, and then there was blackness.

Lewis

THE HEAVENS WEPT as Lewis looked with a face of stone on the flower-covered casket. His mind was gray like the clouds, and he was empty of all emotions except grief. He lifted his eyes toward Lillian, who was clasped in her grandfather's arms, her face buried against his shoulder. The pastor finished her prayer and walked to Lewis and clasped his hands in hers.

"I know you don't understand why this had to happen, but God does. There is a reason of goodness beyond this tragedy."

Lewis averted his eyes from the coffin and stared into the woman's face.

"Don't talk to me about God."

The pastor smiled sadly and gripped his hands. "Lewis, just last week you came forward in church. Lean on God. Its strength will bring you through this."

Lewis shook his head vigorously. "Any God who would kill my wife, I want no part of."

"As humans, we can't understand much of God's plan. But there is a plan. God loves us."

Lewis pulled back his hands. He pointed to the clouds.

"If there is a God, then may He strike me dead right now." He was shouting. "You heard me. Strike me dead, you heartless son of a bitch." As he turned away from the pastor, the people assembled gazed at him in shock.

Lewis walked to his truck and got in. That morning, after being released from the hospital, where he was under sedation, he had refused to ride in the funeral home limousine. From his pocket he took a vial of Valium and washed two pills down with a swig of beer.

People were leaving now, and Lewis saw Beverly's mother, supported by her husband, with Lillian bundled beneath his overcoat. Both his in-laws refused to speak to Lewis.

Pete came up to the window of the truck. "Lewis, I wish to God there was something good to say to you, man. I wish somehow I could help you with this."

"There ain't nothing to say." Lewis stared through the windshield.

"It was an accident. It could have happened to anyone."

"I saw Frank chamber that round. I forgot it. I've never carried a loaded gun in the house."

"You can't blame yourself," Pete said. "It was an accident, man."

"Oh, I know who to blame. Two people."

"Who?"

"Myself and God."

Pete saw two beer cans on Lewis's passenger side. He touched Lewis's arm. "You need to go easy on the drinking. I know you're hurting, but don't make it worse."

"I don't deserve this. I always played by the rules. I walked away from the church, and I got drunk on whiskey one time, and He did this to me."

"You still have Lilly. She needs you even more now."

Lewis shook his head. "I can't bear to look at her. Not after what I did."

"Why don't you come home with me. You need to be with somebody. We have plenty of room."

"No. I need to be alone. I need to go to sleep and not wake up."

"Don't lose it, Lewis. You can bounce back from this. You're a strong man. I ain't never known one stronger."

Lewis cranked his truck. He put it in gear and drove away from the cemetery, ignoring the people who gawked at him, their faces full of pity.

On the way through Chapel Hill, he stopped for supplies—a carton of cigarettes, beer, a case of Absolut. Once at the house, he remained in the driveway and stared at what had been home. Beverly's car was in the carport, Lillian's tricycle beside it. A funeral wreath hung on the front door. He opened a bottle of vodka and drank, and after a few minutes gathered his medicines and headed toward the house. He pulled the wreath down on his way in.

Someone had cleaned the place up. The carpet had been shampooed, his rifle put away God knew where. Lewis carried his load to the bedroom, which smelled of Beverly's perfume. He undressed to his underwear and looked at his reflection in the mirror. Outside he seemed the same, but his insides were gone, stripped from him cleanly.

Lewis lifted the vodka bottle to his mouth, then lit a cigarette and sucked in until his lungs burned. He lay down and fixed his eyes on the ceiling, trying to make his mind as blank as the white paint, as clear as the vodka.

Throughout the afternoon and into the evening he lay there, drinking and smoking and popping Valium and seeking that blankness. Several times the phone rang; the answering machine picked up the calls. A car pulled into the driveway and someone rang the doorbell. Dusk fell and he stared into darkness. The liquor and pills loosened his mind, and he stared through the ceiling and on beyond the roof into the stars.

Somewhere in the middle of a second bottle, Lewis felt himself rise, and soon he was flying higher and higher, swept away by solar wind. He traveled among the stars, between brilliant orbs in the blackness. He rushed upward at the speed of light into the cosmos, passing through . . .

Lewis stood in the front yard. He drank deeply from the bottle, then poured a palmful of liquor on the grass where his wife's blood had spilled. Vines burst from the ground and encircled his feet. They spiraled up his legs, around and around till he was covered in a robe of greenery. Atop his head, they formed a halo. Blooms burst from among the leaves and opened to reveal the bright throats of morning glories. Lewis gazed into one of the blossoms and saw, shimmering as if reflected in water, Beverly's face. He heard her voice, the whisper of a stream.

Love, hear me. I am with you in the fragrance of flowers, in the song of the wind. Open your heart and you will hear me. I am newborn.

My eyes are the stars now, billions that lend me the vision I could not know as woman. My mouth is the moon, wide with wonder at how simple the answers are. My arms stretch from Orion climbing the eastern sky to bright Venus following the sun to sleep. See me clad in the luminous gown of the Milky Way.

My tears are the rain, wept only to bathe your wounds. Lift your face and be cleansed of your grief. I have so very much to tell you, love. We are all children. . . .

The fragrance of the blossoms engulfed him, and years passed while Lewis stood without thoughts or feelings, a piece of the universe and of eternity.

Lewis lifted his face from water. He looked at the vomit in the toilet, shuddered and puked up more red liquid. He wiped his mouth with his hand, then lifted his bottle and gagged down more liquor. Lurching into the bedroom, he raised the bottle like a trumpet. He took another cigarette from the pack, lit it, and drew heavily, before flopping down on the mattress.

Morning now lit the ceiling; the stars he had wandered through had been turned off. The bed was spinning, boring through the floorboards and concrete foundations into the earth. Lewis tasted dirt and worms.

He first smelled the smoke, acrid and nasty, then heard the crackle of flames. Where once the sky had stretched above him he looked into dancing fire.

So be it, he thought. I deserve hell.

He spat toward the flames. The heat mounted quickly and encircled him just as the vines had in the garden. Orange and yellow tendrils burned him and burned him, and he laughed and howled and cursed as he became one with fire.

Ashes

THE MOON STOOD VERTICAL in the heavens above the two huddled men; the frost deepened and glinted like cold fire around them. The lights of mankind from the city grew dim. A rabbit squealed, trapped in the talons of a yellow-eyed owl.

Lewis

I NODDED OFF for a while, and when I woke up, for a few seconds I didn't think Elbridge was breathing. But I shook him a little and he moved, so I knew he was still hanging in there. He's tough. The first time I saw him he was standing on a wall down at Pike Place Market, shouting and preaching. I thought he was just another of the bums, working his scam for whatever the walking blind would throw into his cup. He's strange-looking, mixed-race—part black and God knows what else, with kinky orange hair. Most people would probably call him ugly—hell, I think he's ugly, but I ain't one to talk.

That phrase "Beauty is only skin deep," I know how true it is.

Once, I didn't worry about my own looks. I was no Burt Reynolds, but I looked all right. I know now how life looks from the ugly side. There's a beast in all of us. In some people it lurks on the outside, but it's worse when it lives in your heart. You can always find someone who is uglier than you, or poorer, or dumber. You can think of that unfortunate person and feel better about your own faults, elevate yourself, be cleansed. I have known a beast.

Lewis was first aware of his pulse, steady and measured in his ears. He opened his eye and saw only a muted twilight.

Where am I? he wondered.

Dawn and the sound of his blood: I must be in the tree stand, he thought. In the hour before the first light, waiting on a deer. Yeah, beside the river, and Venus is in the sky and soon the birds will be calling. A big deer that will come to the water, and I will draw him to me in the scope and squeeze down on the trigger . . .

A gunshot. Lewis heard it from deep within his memory, and saw the deer turn and look toward him with those large, unbelieving eyes. The eyes changed, and then the face, as the gun echoed, and he stared at Beverly. In a bolt as terrible as lightning, he remembered.

Oh, God. Let it be a nightmare, he pleaded, and tried to sit up.

"He's waking," the nurse called to the doctor who stood reading a patient's chart. As Lewis struggled to rise, they held him to the bed by his shoulders.

The doctor leaned close to Lewis's ear. "Mr. Calhoon, you're all right. Don't fight it."

Lewis heard voices. He tried to speak but could not open his mouth.

"You're going to be all right, Mr. Calhoon. You're in the burn unit at Memorial Hospital."

Lewis lifted one hand to his face and tore at the bandages.

"Knock him out," the doctor ordered.

The nurse pulled fluid into a needle and pumped it into the IV line. A warm rush spread up Lewis's arm. He fell backward into oblivion.

For two months he had been in the burn unit. He sat in a chair, mirror in hand, as his doctor and a plastic surgeon methodically removed his bandages.

"Lewis," the doctor said, "I want you to understand that plastic surgery can work miracles today."

"I know I look bad. I've felt it with my hands."

"Just remember, five years from now, you'll have a new face."

The doctor unwrapped Lewis from his waist up. The healed skin on his stomach and arms was pink and shiny and hairless. Three fingers on his right hand had been amputated down to the knuckles. His trigger finger was gone. Lewis stared into the mirror as the doctor proceeded. His nipples had been burned off.

"Mr. Calhoon," the plastic surgeon sought to reassure him, "we can start reconstruction this week. There's a lot I can do for you."

Lewis stared into the mirror with fascination and horror as the bandages came off his face. His lips and nose were shriveled, his right ear burned to a nub. His right eye wounded him the most; it was sealed tight, forever sightless. His eyebrows were gone, and most of the hair on his head had been burned away. In his good eye he sought a hint of the man he had been, but the creature in the mirror was as alien as someone from the moon.

The doctor put his hand on Lewis's shoulder. "I know this is tough. But believe me, one day you'll walk in public and no one will give you a second look."

Lewis laid the mirror in his lap. He locked eyes with the doctor. The man blinked, then looked at his feet.

Lewis checked the clock again, dreading the imminent visit from Pete and the lawyer who handled his company. He had shut out the world for eight weeks, but he had to confront it now. Life for him stopped on that Saturday when the gun went off, while for everyone else, the sun rose and set, and time passed. Real time was about to come walking through Lewis's door, like it or not. When he heard the knock on the door, he turned toward the window.

"Come in," he shouted. The door opened, and there were footsteps on the smooth floor. Silence, then Pete's voice.

"Boss man? That you?"

Turning slowly from the window, Lewis swept the faces of his visitors.

"Lewis." Pete took a step forward, his eyes fixed on his friend's face. "Buddy, it's good to see you." He extended his hand.

Lewis moved his right arm, then remembered his fingers. He put out his left and awkwardly shook hands.

"Boss man, it's good to see you."

"It's been a while." Lewis nodded toward the lawyer. "Hello, Ben."

"Hello, Lewis."

He pointed toward two chairs. "Sit down. I guess we have some business to discuss."

The lawyer cleared his throat and shuffled through his papers. "I hate to talk about these things now, but we have to."

"I understand. I know I ain't been too communicative lately."

"Well, you had good reason."

"How bad off is the company?"

"Pretty bad. You know how banks are. They don't like to wait on loan payments."

"Don't I know."

"Well, I think bankruptcy is about our only option. With the insurance money from . . . from . . ."

"I know from where."

"Well, I can keep a nest egg for you. You can start over."

"Sell what you can," Lewis told the lawyer. "Let the bank take the rest. I'm through with it."

Pete sat forward in his chair. "Boss man, we can start over. I'll stick with you. I know Jimmy will too. We started out little, and we can do it again."

Lewis held out his right hand. "Think that can hold a hammer?"

"I'll swing the hammer. You still got your brain."

"It ain't the same neither."

"Man, you still have Lilly," Pete said. "You've got to support her."

Lewis's eye was flat; he saw something distant in his mind. "She's with her grandparents. She's better off with them."

"She needs her daddy." Pete brushed his hand

through his hair. "Lewis, I never admired a man more than you. You've always been like a hero to me. You can rise up from this. You can beat it, and we'll start over."

"I can't bring Beverly back."

Silence hung thick for several seconds. "When you getting out of here?" Pete asked. "When can you leave?"

Lewis sighed deeply. "Anytime. All I got to do is put my hand on the door and open it and walk through."

Lewis stood at the threshold, waiting to open the door. He looked into the night sky, at the stars sharp in the chill air; in his hands was his rifle, and he clicked the safety on and off. He awaited the dawn, when he could see the river and know the deer were up and moving.

Just past midnight, he had walked away from the burn unit. He ignored the cold and marched the three miles to his house, wearing only his pajamas and robe, stretching muscles that had not been used for weeks. The bedroom had been gutted by the fire, but he found his rifle where Pete had stowed it with his hunting clothes. His truck keys were still under the seat of the cab. In the hour before the first light, he arrived at the sandbar where he had killed the twelve-pointer.

Lewis watched the day arrive, as spokes of pink in the east. The world was different through one eye—like a postcard, lacking the depth two eyes afforded—but still beautiful after he'd been in the hospital for so long. He gulped in great breaths of air, fruited by the scent of the river, of frost and dry leaves, of animals and birds. A breeze blew as the sun lifted, cool on the virgin skin of his face. Born of earth and water, he had been forged by fire into something new. The wind on his face cooled the fire.

After he clicked off the safety of his rifle and chambered a round, Lewis tilted his face toward the sky and yelled. "You think all this was fair to do to a man who just wasn't ready to be baptized?"

With the sun only minutes below the horizon, the sky glowed. Lewis stared into that fire and wondered what was ahead. If he was lucky, there would be only darkness and an endless peace. His body would decompose here on this sand, and his dust would blow onto the water and eventually wash out to sea. After years, his atoms would drift in every ocean on earth. Or maybe he would walk through that door into hell. At least in his eternal damnation he would be in a place where God did not hold domain.

He put the rifle barrel under his chin, and found he could just reach the trigger with his thumb. He closed his eye and thought of a big buck in the crosshairs of his scope, in a time when he had held control. Now he held the final control.

His throat was dry, and whatever followed, oblivion or torment, he wanted once more to taste cold water. He leaned the rifle against a tree and fell to his knees in the sand, then lapped at the river like an animal. When he lifted his face, water dripped from his chin and cast ripples on the surface. He gazed at the ripples, and as they ceased, the water became a mirror and reflected his scars. He stared with disgust at the image that seemed as much animal as man, and a hate welled inside him, crackling and spitting like brimstone.

Lewis stood slowly. His head shook back and forth as realization flooded his mind. *That's what He wants you to do. Kill yourself and be totally defeated. Erased from the world. I didn't deserve this. Not for walking out of a church. I played by the rules.*

He lifted his rifle and fired into the sky. "You started

this, you bastard! You're going to have to finish it!" He chambered another round and another, and fired until the magazine was empty. Then he threw his rifle in the middle of the river.

Lewis shivered, aware of the cold surrounding him. He drew his knees up and wrapped his arms tighter around his shoulders. His head throbbed, and the concrete against his cheek felt like rough ice; the air smelled of urine and cigarette smoke. Lewis could hear men stirring, the rasp of matches being struck, the sound of someone emptying his bladder.

The past days were a blur to Lewis. He remembered leaving the river and driving to the bank, where he cashed out what was left in his checking account. He stocked up on vodka, then drove westward. He retained mere fragments of his journey—the miles he had traveled; the nights he had slept in the driver's seat, parked at rest stops; the mornings he had woken sick and hurting, only to gulp down enough liquor to get him through another day on the interstate. He had no idea where he was going; just that three thousand miles lay between him and the Pacific Ocean.

Lewis cracked open his eye and sat up. A dozen men filled the crowded cell, all of them sullen-looking. Several stared at him; no one spoke.

The cell door opened, and the jailer entered. He read a few names from a list and told those men to follow him out. Across the cell, Lewis noticed a skinny man with gray hair and bad teeth. He caught the man's eyes, and the old guy held the gaze. Lewis stood and walked to the commode and let go a stream of urine.

Over the next hour, the jailer came and called for more men, until only Lewis and the skinny man were left. As the jailer was about to leave again, Lewis asked, "What you got me charged with?"

"Drunk driving and resisting arrest."

"How do I get out of here?"

"That might be a trick. You had a little over a hundred dollars in your wallet. Your bail is set at two thousand."

"Can't I use my truck as bond?"

"That truck was flagged on the computers by a bank back in North Carolina. It's been repossessed."

"Well, how the fuck do I get two thousand dollars?"

"That's your big riddle, mister."

The jailer closed the door. Lewis rested his head against the wall and shut his eye. He needed a drink bad. When he opened his eye, he saw the skinny man staring. "What're you looking at?" he growled.

After a while, the jailer appeared with two plastic trays, each of which held a plate with a lump of scrambled eggs, two strips of bacon, and a slice of bread, a plastic spoon, and a paper cup filled with black coffee. He set the trays on the bench. "If you want to eat, it's here."

The skinny man hurried over and picked up one of the trays. He put it on his lap and began shoveling the food into his mouth. Lewis watched the man clean the plate in a minute.

"You going to eat?" he asked.

Lewis shook his head.

"You care if I have yours?"

Lewis looked at the grease on the man's chin. "Be my guest."

The jailer returned this time with another man, who looked Lewis up and down. "Damn it, Pop," the man told Lewis's cellmate, "I'm getting tired of bailing you out of jail every Sunday morning."

The skinny man crammed what was left of the food

into his mouth. "This is the last time, Mr. Brodie. It won't happen again." He set the tray down and rushed through the doorway.

Lewis heard muffled voices. When the door opened again after a few minutes, the man named Brodie entered. He narrowed one eye in thought. "What happened to you?"

"None of your damn business."

"I might be able to get you out of here. You'll have to pay me back, though."

"How am I gonna pay you back?"

"I'm a businessman. I have a job where I think you'd fit right in."

The morning sun filtered through the tattered gauze curtain on the window above Lewis's bed. The trailer wasn't rocking, so he knew the carnival had reached the next town.

Lewis reached for his cigarettes from the nightstand. He lit one and sucked in, then exhaled in a long blue stream. After putting the cigarette in a jar lid, he half filled a cup with vodka and drank it straight down.

He lay back and closed his eye and waited for the alcohol to kick in. Popov wasn't as smooth as Absolut, but it was much cheaper and did the same job. The Reptile Man wasn't Lewis Calhoon either.

Lewis liked traveling between cities. When he was in the pit, he had to keep some sort of restraint. But when he came out of the pit on Saturday night, he usually had a day and a half before the roadies tore everything down and the carnival drove off and set up again. Riding at night was especially good. He'd stoke his belly with vodka and lie in bed and watch the highway lights flash through the window. Somewhere near the end of a bottle, the alcohol and the undulation of the moving trailer would put him to sleep, and for hours he'd cease to exist.

The alcohol was crawling across Lewis's forehead. He wondered what town they were in; they could be in another state by now. Ten, his wristwatch said: still time to make the morning service. He poured another drink and heaved to his feet. Outside the window he could see flat ground to the horizon, with only a few trees. They were deep in the Midwest. About a mile away was the skyline of a town. Two church steeples rose above the other buildings, fingers pointing the way to heaven. Wild flowers dotted the green grass around the trailer. He had looked out over snow the past week, and for much of the winter he spent with the carnival. The work fed him, paid him enough to stay drunk, gave him a bed to pass out in. But what he needed most from it was the shocked look in the eyes of the people who came to see him.

Standing straight, Lewis felt his head brush the ceiling of the trailer. The compact room could hold only a bed and nightstand, a small kitchenette, and an even smaller toilet. His trailer and two others, pulled in a line behind a truck, carried the featured freaks of the Brodie Brothers Carnival. Lewis's was in the rear, the Fat Lady's ahead of his, and Harry the Human Pincushion's up front.

Lewis relieved himself in the toilet; the alcohol was kicking in good. He stooped in front of the refrigerator and took out a jug of orange juice and three eggs, then wiped out a frying pan, his only pan, with an old washcloth, poured in a little oil, and turned on the gas.

He fried his eggs sunny-side up, slid them onto a paper plate, and sprinkled on salt and pepper, then sat on his bed to eat. After a glass of juice, he poured himself a big shot of vodka. He was getting back to that place where thought and emotion were as distant as stars.

Lewis remained outside the door of the church and took another drag on his cigarette. He could hear the congregation finishing "Just As I Am," and next the words of the preacher.

"Won't you come now, this very minute. Won't you come to Jesus. Tomorrow might be too late."

In his mind, Lewis could imagine the scene inside the church: a painting of the river Jordan in the baptistery, the preacher with his head tilted toward the ceiling, the congregation standing with hymnals in hand.

"One more verse," he heard the preacher say. The organ started up again, low and mournful. "Just step out into the aisle. People will let you by. Come home to the Lord."

Lewis knew the anguish of the liars and adulterers and drinkers, of teenagers trying to push from their minds the beer and pot and last night's session in the backseat, even of children who did not yet know how to read but were convinced they were filled with sin.

"Jesus is waiting," the preacher continued. "He's waiting for you."

Lewis flicked his cigarette onto the concrete, opened the heavy wooden door, and started down the aisle. He fixed his eye on the preacher as he came forward. The congregation, people in suits and dresses, scrubbed clean of the week's toil, turned to look at Lewis when he passed each row; they saw only the back of his head. As he approached the altar, the preacher's smile disappeared and his eyes widened. The elderly woman playing the organ glanced up, her mouth dropped open, and she paused in the music, then started over. Lewis mounted the two steps to the altar; the preacher took a step backward. Lewis slowly faced the congregation. The organ stopped.

"Do you . . . do you wish to accept Jesus Christ?" the preacher asked.

Lewis waited before shaking his head. "No." He scanned the congregation; many of the people averted their gaze from the scars, the fierce one-eyed glare. He walked down from the altar and toward the door, looking straight ahead, at that place only he could see.

On Monday at five till noon, Lewis stood beside his pit. He unbuttoned his shirt and hung it by the collar on a nail driven into a tent pole, then slipped his watch off and dropped it into the pocket of his ragged camo trousers. Next, he turned the kerosene heater up full blast.

Lewis surveyed the interior of the tent. On a shelf to one side were the pickled freaks in jars—a human fetus with three legs, a piglet with two heads, a frog with no front legs, all of them gray, years dead. A stuffed two-headed calf stood on a low platform, a fake shrunken head sat atop a wooden table, and a cork board covered with photographs of Siamese twins, bearded women, and other abnormalities awaited spectators at the entrance. Lewis heard the barker outside begin his spiel.

"Mother Nature's mistakes!" he proclaimed. "Oddities of creation that you will not believe until you see them with your naked eye. The Reptile Man, half human, half snake, brought back from an expedition in the Amazon. The Fat Lady, born weighing eight pounds, she now tips the scales at more than a quarter-ton. Harry the Human Pincushion, born without the sensation of pain, he pierces his body with instruments of steel."

Frances, the Fat Lady, sat on her large wooden throne, in a bright pink dress with lace and ribbons, her face heavily made-up, her lips and nails painted red. In her lap rested one of the numerous sweaters she knitted for the roadies.

Harry sat cross-legged on a wooden platform, his eyes shut, his mind stretched between the comforts of yoga and hashish.

"Mother Nature's unfortunate children," the barker called out, "better never born. No tricks, no mirrors. Live before your very eyes."

Lewis's pit was a box formed of four sheets of plywood nailed together at the edges. The wood had been garishly painted on the exterior with a design of snakes draped over jungle vines. On the side facing the tent entrance was painted a snake man, human from the waist above, reptile below, his open mouth revealing long white fangs. With a minute to go, Lewis took his ice cooler—a fifth of vodka, a pack of cigarettes, two cans of Vienna sausages inside—stepped over the side of the box, and sat with his back against the rear wall. He poured some vodka into a paper cup and drank it down. There was a show at the top of every hour, and he would be sitting in the pit until around midnight; by then the fifth would be empty. He would stagger back to his trailer, fall into bed, and do it all again the next day.

"It's showtime," the barker went on. "Get your tickets now. You'll thank the good Lord you were born normal."

Lewis took his plastic fangs from his pocket and put them in his mouth.

*

"Look at that ugly mother!" a man exclaimed.

"Hush," his wife answered. "It might be able to hear."

Lewis gave the people a once-over. During the months he had listened to the hisses and gasps and comments of hundreds of people, he had learned to decipher the wrinkles and scars on their faces. Their thoughts were reflected in their eyes, and he could speculate on their histories, their hopes, their successes and failures, as just more chapters in a long, sad book. . . .

Squinting at Lewis was a man wearing a bolo tie with fake turquoise. He was a parts salesman for farm equipment in three states, and he spent his nights in cheap motels, as often as possible with cheap women. His wife was short and mousy; makeup only partially hid the bruise under her eye. She spent her lonely nights looking at *Better Homes and Gardens,* wishing and dreaming

"God—look at that!" A teenage boy tightened his arm around his girlfriend's small waist. She snuggled closer, and thought of the night before, and what they had done at the drive-in. He had said that he loved her, that he would hurt down there if she wouldn't let him. He wouldn't say he loved her if he didn't mean it. The boy felt the warmth of her waist and wondered how many times he'd have to throw a softball through a tire before he won her a stuffed bear, and then they could leave, and go to the dirt road beside the gravel pit, where you could hear the frogs debate. He'd remind her of the dollars he'd spent, and if that didn't work, he'd say he loved her.

"Do you think it's real?" a kid asked. He smoked cigarettes behind the barn and kept *Penthouse* pictures in a buried mason jar. Last week, when they'd had the tornado warning, he'd prayed and sworn he would throw the pictures away, but the tornado passed over, and anyway, that was last week.

A sign above Lewis's pit read: TOSS MONEY TO SEE IT MOVE. The man with the bolo tie threw a nickel, which bounced off the Reptile Man's head.

"I don't think it's real," the kid decided.

The people who came to see the freaks were much the same town to town, ordinary people with ordinary hopes and fears and problems. They'd huddle around Harry and watch him pierce his tongue and cheeks with pins and nails. For the adolescent girl who'd had her ears pierced against her father's wishes, the sight of the man mutilating himself was comforting. The gold spheres on her own earlobes were small, and in time her daddy would realize how pretty they were. The head-banger with orange-spiked hair watched with fascination as Harry pushed the nail through his skin. The head-banger liked to run a little coke up his arm on occasion, but that was harmless compared with what this freak was doing.

The nineteen-year-old mother of two observed the Fat Lady with almost a feeling of joy. The young mother had weighed a hundred twenty when Joey had gotten her pregnant, but now she was carrying about forty extra pounds. Babies did that to you, and so did sitting around the house all day. But she wasn't fat, she realized now; she was as slender as a fawn, next to that made-up blob sitting in that chair. In fact, she could continue to enjoy her little pleasure right now, a bag of potato chips.

When you looked down into the pit at that disgusting Reptile Man, many of these people thought, your sins were forgiven. Few if any believed the creature was really part reptile, but they knew that whatever had befallen it was tragic.

He must have done something pretty horrible, something horrible and wicked, for God to have done that to him, the man with the bolo tie reasoned. He himself was living pretty good, he reckoned. All he had was an ulcer, and sometimes he got the gout. He and the Lord got along all right.

The man's wife touched the bruise under her eye, and already the swelling seemed to be gone. She realized now that it had been okay for her to buy that rug for the living room without telling her husband. He hadn't meant to hit her; it was probably an accident. God would punish you when you sinned, and this man sitting in the box must have sinned badly. Or maybe his father had sinned and brought it on him. Must have done something real bad.

Doing things in the backseat, smoking cigarettes behind the barn, telling a lie here and there, using some lonely man or woman for the night—that was small stuff when people looked at the freaks. Suddenly they felt washed clean; younger and prettier and healthier . . . damn near perfect.

"He didn't move," the kid said. "I think he's dead."

The man with the bolo tie now fished a quarter from his pocket. He squinted with one eye and aimed, then threw the coin toward Lewis. It struck his forehead and stung, and he opened his eye. The Reptile Man gaped, showed fangs and bellowed. The ring of people scrambled backward, startled; some laughed, a few hurried for the exit. Yet some of them looked purified, as if walking out of church on Sunday.

When all the people had left, Lewis took his bottle from the cooler. Soon enough the barker would start up again, and a new crowd would gather, different faces, ages, lives, but everyone there for the same thing.

You don't know nothing about me, Lewis thought.

None of you know the slightest thing about me, and you love me and hate me at the same time. I was good. I was all-conference. I was handsome and had a wife and a baby girl. I built houses and employed people. You'd never believe me if I told you, because you'd know it could happen to you and you and you. I am the nigger and the faggot and the whore and the fat girl in grade school. I am the wimp who can't catch a softball and the bum sitting with his bottle of wine. I am the man ahead of you in the grocery line paying with food stamps, and the young man behind you bald from chemotherapy. But you're not me—yet. Not yet, motherfuckers, and Yet never comes to some people, while some people it takes out young.

Weeks passed and spring became summer. The carnival worked its way farther west, across land so flat that Lewis could look miles back toward where he came from. He hated the empty plains, for in those vast expanses he sometimes felt the pull of home, and had memories he no longer desired.

But Lewis had found a way to take charge. He knew now what his father had come to know: When the world was too wrong to fix, you could blot it out with liquor. You could slide under that warm blanket, and what had once mattered didn't anymore. Lewis could raise his bottle and lay another brick in the wall he was building.

The last show for this day had ended. Lewis stood outside Frances's trailer door, once again trying to decide whether he should knock. She expected him now every Wednesday night. Fire had not changed him from the waist down, and despite the liquor, he still felt the need. Finally he knocked, opened the unlocked door, and went inside.

Frances's trailer was larger than his, and nicely furnished. A queen-sized bed covered with an elaborate patchwork quilt filled much of the room. Hanging on one wall was a print of van Gogh's *Starry Night;* on another, a poster of Monet's *Water Lilies.* Schubert played on the stereo, and a single scented candle burned in a pewter holder.

Lewis sat down in a stuffed chair and waited several minutes before Frances emerged from her bathroom. She wore a long silk gown, and had tied back her hair with ribbons; her makeup was perfect. She had a pretty face and would have been altogether attractive if a thyroid problem hadn't swollen her to more than five hundred pounds. She smiled sadly as she knelt on the floor in front of Lewis. Slowly she unfastened his belt, then unzipped his pants and slid his trousers down. Looking into his face, she took his penis into her hand and squeezed it.

"I'm a beautiful woman," she said in a dreamy voice. "I weigh only a hundred and ten pounds, and I have a fiancé, and we're going to get married."

Lewis closed his eyes and rested his head against the back of the chair.

"I'm a tiny young girl, and all the boys like me and send me flowers and candy, but I don't eat the candy. I have long, slender legs, and my stomach is firm and flat. My breasts are small, but they stand out."

Frances began to stroke him with one hand, her other hand between her legs. "My fiancé got in a fight the other night with a man who whistled at me. He's very jealous. Sometimes I wish I weren't so beautiful."

She took him in her mouth then, and the trailer rocked with her motion.

*

Lewis left Frances's trailer for his own, and with a blanket and pillow and his bottle went to lie under the stars. The carnival was set up far from any large city, and the Milky Way arched across the heavens like a midnight rainbow. Lewis stared into the haze of the galaxy. Stars millions and millions of miles apart, yet looking as close together as pebbles on a beach. His grief and anger were as boundless as the black sky—he was living them, and meant to ride them until the God who had taken his wife took him too.

He awoke with the sun burning through his eyelid. Someone touched his shoulder. He opened his eye and looked up at Frances.

"You all right?" she asked.

He rubbed his face. His clothes were wet with dew, an empty bottle lay beside him. "Yeah, yeah, I'm all right."

"You shouldn't drink like you do, Lewis. You're going to kill yourself."

"I got a lot to live for."

"You got your life. We could be friends. We could talk. You drink so much you're usually passed out."

Lewis's knees creaked when he stood up, and his head hurt. He wondered how low he was getting on vodka. He'd have to send one of the roadies to the liquor store. You never knew when a dry town might come along.

"When you look at me, what do you see?" he asked Frances.

"I see a man who's been hurt bad. I see a man who's still trying to hurt himself."

"I'm not a man no more. I'm a fucking reptile. Ain't you ever read my sign?"

"You are a man, Lewis. Just like I'm a woman. It doesn't matter what we look like on the outside."

Lewis shook his head. "No, I'm not a man. I stopped being that one day." He turned and walked toward his trailer. "It was years and years and years ago."

The carnival left the plains, moved on over the Rockies, into Idaho, and eventually to the dry flatlands of eastern Washington. Lewis measured his days by bottles and sat deep inside his shell surrounded by the same people he had seen in Georgia and Illinois. The John Deere and Purina caps had been replaced by cowboy hats, but the faces underneath were the same, with the same look of horror and thankfulness. Lewis no longer kept his bottle inside the cooler; now he jammed it between his legs and sat slouched over it.

Lewis lay outside and gazed into the purple night sky. Above the high Washington desert, the stars burned brighter than any he had ever seen, sharp as pinholes in a sheet of black paper held toward the sun. The land was level again, but Lewis did not feel the pull of memories. He had watched as the caravan wound through the mountains, then descended into valleys. A high wall now stood between him and the man he had once been. As liquor laid brick after brick each day against his memory, it seemed the earth too conspired with walls higher than clouds.

Lewis took several gulps from his bottle. The words from a song came into his head. "I'm not the man they think I am," he whispered. "I'm a rocket maaannnnn."

He chuckled, then stopped abruptly. Am I a rocket man, he asked himself, rocketed off to some new world?

Dim in his memory now were the scent of long-leaf pine, the smell of rain during a summer storm, the tang of tobacco being cured. He could hardly differentiate the sharp crack of a rifle shot from the long, slow rumble of thunder. People and images from the past had all become distant—little Lillian and the kids who gawked at him, Beverly's eyes and the slain buck. Lewis felt alcohol, good and strong in his blood, and knew it would be easy to drift into sleep. Here in this high country the cold would come and take him.

Lewis struggled to his feet. He looked toward the eastern horizon, then into the sky above.

"You're taking your time, old boy," he shouted. "You're taking your fucking time to kill me, old man."

Lewis wove a crooked path across the dry dirt toward his trailer. Overhead, the Milky Way pointed to the west and the sea.

Late one night, Lewis was awakened by the low-geared growl of the truck. His ears were popping and he could hear the engines straining, so he knew they were crossing mountains again. Through the window he could see only a string of lights in the dark as the caravan threaded its way up a steep curve.

More mountains—Lewis felt a strange excitement. They were crossing rock again, and maybe beyond this wall his past would cease to exist. He let the whine of the gears put him back to sleep.

A pure, clean light danced across the linoleum floor of the trailer. Lewis heard the roadies setting up, generators roaring, sledgehammers clanging, men shouting. He pulled himself out of bed, walked to the door, and swung it open.

"God damn!" He had never seen such mountains.

To the east before him, the land sloped skyward, covered with a thick forest of spruce. A few miles beyond, the world stood vertical, a craggy, purple-and-gray wall topped with snow. To the south was an even larger mountain, silent and ominous and glowing in the sunlight. To the west, the land dropped sharply toward a brilliant blue bay, and across it were more jagged mountains, erect and solid, their snow caps like diamonds in the sun.

"Where the hell we at?" Lewis asked a roadie.

"Outside Seattle." The roadie pointed to a city skyline on the shores of the bay.

Lewis turned a complete circle. He was aware of being in a gigantic granite bowl, shut solidly behind rock walls so high he wondered how the caravan could have arrived here.

"This is it," he murmured to himself. "I'm here. Ain't nothing can follow me over that wall."

Lewis returned to his trailer. From a hole in the underside of his mattress, he pulled out a sock, inside of which was a roll of bills. He counted slowly: fifty-seven dollars, all he had to show for months of baring his face, the rest of his earnings gone for booze. Lewis folded the money and put it in his pocket, then pulled a canvas duffel from underneath the bed. He packed it with his few clothes and two full fifths of vodka, shouldered it, and went outside.

The tents were going up fast: another week in another town for the carnival. Lewis might have searched the horizon for church steeples, but the mountains so dwarfed the architecture of humans that he felt he already stood inside a great cathedral. He heard music from Frances's trailer, and it reminded him of an invitational hymn.

"Here I am, motherfuckers," he said. "Look upon me and live."

To his left, Lewis saw a patch of wild flowers growing in a rotten stump. He leaned and picked a handful, and went to Frances's trailer and laid them on the top step. And there, for once knowing that he would not knock, he turned and began walking away from the carnival and from mankind and from the face of the earth.

Lewis had gone less than a mile when he saw a cab on the side of the road. Inside sat an Asian man, his head against the back of the driver's seat, his eyes closed. Lewis rapped on the window, and the man jumped when he saw what stood outside.

"I need a ride."

"You—you got money?"

Lewis showed the man some bills, and the cabbie unlocked the rear door. Lewis threw his bag in, then himself.

The cabbie stared into the rearview mirror. "Where you go?" he asked.

Lewis reached into his bag, pulled out a bottle, and took a long swallow. "Where do you think I want to go?"

"What say?"

"Turn around and look at me," Lewis demanded.

The cabbie hesitated, then obeyed. He stared into Lewis's eye.

Lewis tipped the bottle again. "Where in this town would a man like me want to go?"

The cabbie blinked repeatedly. "Pioneer Square. You go Pioneer Square."

"Drive on, Jack."

Elbridge

WHEN I WAS IN THE HOSPITAL, I had a vision. I stood at the base of this great big mountain range, looking up toward the peaks. I had to go over them mountains. I wasn't sure why, but I had come miles and miles and couldn't stop now. I took a step, and another one, but the ground moved toward me like I was walking the wrong way up an escalator. I started running, and the ground slid faster and faster toward me. Seemed like hours and hours I ran, and didn't gain a yard. Finally I stopped and looked down at my hands, and there in them was my shotgun. I raised it toward the mountains and fired, and those mountains tore like a sheet of paper and fell to each side with a roar. All of a sudden there was cool wind blowing on my face and through that gap in the mountains I saw nothing but blue, stretching to the horizon. It wasn't a dream; it was a real vision.

When I came out of the coma, I knew Rita and the girls were dead. I knew it before the chaplain came and sat down beside me. I accepted it and tried not to question why. The social worker told me their remains had been buried together in a common grave.

A month in intensive care, then three months in another room, and eventually the infections and fevers quit.

"You've lost about half your capacity to absorb oxygen," the doctor said. "The damage is bad."

"Will it get worse?" I asked.

The doctor nodded. "Possibly."

"Will it kill me?"

He stared at his clipboard. "You might live for years, Elbridge. More realistically, you'll probably get another infection before too long, and maybe your lungs won't be strong enough to handle it."

"Soon?"

"Only God knows that."

At the graveyard, I kneeled in front of the headstone where Rita and the girls were buried. Just one word was on it: Snipes. They could at least have put their first names too. "I tried to go in that fire, Rita," I whispered. "I tried to go right in, but it wasn't meant. I would have got y'all out, or burned right up with you. But it wasn't meant."

I cried a little while, then slipped my wedding band from my finger and buried it in a little hole atop the grave. Then I stood and looked into the sky. "I'm your servant, Lord. Lead me." I closed my eyes and turned around and around until I was dizzy. When I opened my eyes, I could tell by the sun that I was facing northwest. I had a satchel with one change of clothes and a sleeping bag, and one hundred dollars from Social Services in my pocket. I started walking.

I hitched a bunch of rides toward the Northwest, on interstates and county roads, in semis and cars and in the beds of pickups. Inside my brain, like a color picture, was the vision I'd seen, those high mountains and that blue that went forever beyond them. I knew I had to go over them mountains, because an answer waited for me there.

I never could have imagined how big and different the country was beyond the Appalachians. The land flattened out and the sky got bigger. The people were different too, like the man driving a semi who picked me up one morning. He was black as tar and had a gold tooth in the front.

"What tribe are you from?" he asked after we had rode awhile.

"I ain't from no tribe."

"I am from Sudan. There we all know what tribe we are from. Every man is from a tribe. He needs to know where he comes from."

"I know where I'm going," I told him. "That's all that matters to me." I didn't know about no special tribes. This guy looked to me like any of a hundred niggers I'd seen with their butts turned up in a tobacco field. I rode with him all the way into St. Louis. I thought my eyes would pop out when we drove over the Mississippi. I didn't know a river could be so wide.

"What's that?" I said. I saw this big silver thing.

"That's the Gateway Arch."

"Gateway to what?"

"Gateway to the West, man."

That arch rose like a big door, and I knew right then I was entering a land I'd probably never come out of.

I was in Kansas when the hippies picked me up. Two men and two women, all of them with long hair and beads and paint splashed over their clothes, riding in a van. I told the guy driving my name; he said he was Thor, and the woman riding shotgun said she was Moonbeam. The other two were sleeping on the floor in the back.

"Where y'all going?" I asked, when we had gone about a mile.

Thor looked at me in the mirror. "We're following the Dead."

A jolt shot through my belly. I didn't need any more strange people. Just the day before, a man had picked me up and asked if I wanted a blow job. I told him no, and he let me out at the next exit ramp.

"What dead?"

Moonbeam turned to me. Her hair was purple. "We're Deadheads. You know, people who follow the Grateful Dead."

"I think I might get out here," I told her.

She laughed. "It's a band. We're going to a concert in Denver." She slid a tape into the player and loud music started up. She bobbed her head at me.

Around noontime Thor pulled in at a rest stop. I was getting my bag to leave when Moonbeam asked me to stay for lunch. They seemed like harmless people, and free food was hard to turn down, so I thanked her for the offer.

Moonbeam loaded a picnic table with stuff, food I'd never seen before. "Help yourself," she said, and told me what everything was: "Tabbouleh, lentils, sprout salad, hummus, and pita. All chemical-free, all the ingredients straight from the earth."

Straight from the earth? I'd never eaten nothing that wasn't from the earth. Even the doves I liked to shoot were earth creatures. I lowered my head and said a quick prayer before I ate anything. The food tasted all right, but it needed salt. I noticed the hippies ate mostly with their fingers.

"Where are you traveling?" Thor asked me.

"To some mountains. They're in the Northwest."

He nodded. "What's in the mountains?"

"It's on the other side of the mountains. There's something there for me. I don't know what yet."

Thor nodded again, real slow. He looked up from his plate. "You're on a quest."

Moonbeam took some brownies from a plastic sack. "You want a brownie, Elbridge? They're good for the head."

Better good for my stomach, I thought. At least that was food I recognized. "Yes, ma'am."

She handed me one. It wasn't as good as the brownies Rita used to make, and it smelled like dried fescue hay, but I ate it anyhow. The hippies who had been in the back of the van got up from the table and walked over to a patch of grass. They sat down facing each other, crossed their legs, and closed their eyes.

"What are they doing?" I asked Moonbeam.

"They're meditating. You ever meditate?"

"Is it like praying? I pray a lot."

"It's kind of like praying. Have you heard of Zen?"

"No."

"It's an Eastern religion. See, we're all on a wheel, and we're all trying to get to the center of the wheel, where we'll find Nirvana."

"What's Nirvana?"

"Total peace."

"That sounds like heaven."

"It is, in a way. But it's not like you sit around and play a harp. You become like the air, part of the cosmos, a particle of the godhead."

Warning bells went off in my brain. "That ain't heaven. Heaven is a place you go. There's people there.

Christian people. My children, my wife . . ." I shook my head. "God is in heaven."

Moonbeam smiled at me. "That's right, Elbridge."

After we'd been back on the road some miles, my face started feeling funny. First there was a tickle right between my eyes; it spread down my body till my toes itched. I could hear my eyelashes when I blinked, like wind in willow branches. Thor turned on some music, and it was real clear, as if the voices had separated from the guitars. The paint on Moonbeam's shirt glowed like fire.

I stared at the highway. I felt like the van was sitting still and the whole earth was sliding by. Rain began falling, the drops splatting the windows like little bombs. The van seemed long as a school bus. I held up my hand, and it looked to be two yards away.

Moonbeam smiled at me. "Are you stoned yet, Elbridge?" Her voice came out of a deep well and echoed after her lips had stopped moving.

"Stoned?"

"Are you high yet? From the hash brownies?"

"Hash?" The only hash I knew was corned beef hash.

"You know, like pot."

I knew pot. A lot of the wetbacks had smoked it in the fields. It was supposed to make you crazy. But I didn't feel crazy, I felt as loose as the water on the windshield. I was flying, the rain and the whole world passing under me. Moonbeam's voice played over and over in my head: "We're all on a wheel . . . trying to get to the center." A semi went by, and I watched the tires spinning, slinging rain outward like pinwheels. I looked at the clouds and remembered we were in Kansas, and thought about *The Wizard of Oz* and how I'd watched it with Cindy and Connie. I felt like Dorothy: that tornado had picked me up too and dropped me into a world where the old rules didn't apply.

I hitched my way up Colorado, then crossed into Wyoming and over the Rockies. The land went flat again, the snow changed to rock and dust. In Idaho, a man hauling cows picked me up, and I helped him drive. He took me to his ranch, and I helped him unload, and he paid me and let me stay the night. He was a Mormon and had three wives. I wanted to tell him that was wrong, but he had fed me and paid me, and I couldn't find the words.

Most nights I just unrolled my sleeping bag behind a bush near the road. I couldn't get over the hugeness of the sky above me, the brightness of the stars; they made me dizzy. Storms would boil up and hide the stars yet still be miles and miles away, so far away I couldn't hear the thunder. Back home, the whole universe had seemed within shouting distance. Out here, a man could have fired a rifle and the bullet would have passed through nothing but air till it dropped. I said my prayers every night, but it bothered me that my words were sucked into that big sky, as unnoticed as a glassful of water poured in a river. God's ear had seemed much closer at home, when I was on my knees under a ceiling. Sometimes when I was drifting off, I'd remember Moonbeam talking about the great wheel and see how the sky turned above me, and then I'd stop worrying and wondering about it all and just sleep.

I was outside Spokane, about to give up for the day and hunt for a place to sleep, when a car swerved over and stopped. I climbed into an old Cutlass. There were two guys in the front seat, one with long hair and a beard, the other, who was driving, with a shaved head. They both had beers in their hands, and the back floorboard was stacked with empties.

"You guys going west?" I asked.

"Yeah."

"I'm Elbridge Snipes."

Neither of them answered. The car smelled of beer and sweat and cigarettes. I already wished it hadn't stopped.

"You want a beer, man?" the hairy one asked.

"I don't drink."

The guy laughed, then lifted his can and chugged it. "I never met anybody that didn't drink." He squinted at me through his cigarette smoke. "What's your pedigree, man?"

"What you mean?"

"I mean, what the fuck race are you? You got a flat nose and big lips and blue eyes, and your hair is orange."

I felt anger in my gut, so I took a long breath. "I'm just a man." I shrugged.

"Just a man!" The guy laughed again. "You look like you're parts of several men."

Dark was coming, and I decided then to get out as soon as the car stopped. A few miles down the highway, the driver shot into an exit ramp, and I felt some relief. But instead of stopping at the service station, he went on a road that led into the country.

"I need to get out here," I said.

"I thought you wanted a ride," the driver said.

"I need to stay on the interstate."

"This is a shortcut. We'll get back on the interstate."

The moon was up when he braked beside the road. The hairy guy got out and opened my door. "You said you wanted out, dude."

All I saw was darkness beyond the headlights, but I wasn't about to complain. "Thanks, guys." I leaned over and was slipping through the door when hands gripped my collar and threw me to the ground. I felt gravel cut into my knees, and cold metal against my temple.

"You got any money, half-breed?"

"No."

"Don't make me blow your fucking brains out."

The hairy one pushed the gun harder against my head. I started praying. The other guy pulled my wallet from my pocket.

"A fucking twenty," he growled.

"A cheap half-breed," the hairy guy said. "Take your clothes off."

I twisted away and stood facing him. "You can shoot me if you want to. I ain't giving you nothing else." I was blinded by a flashlight, and then felt something move to my side. I swung into the air, and something hard crashed into the back of my neck. I swung again and turned, only to get a knee in the belly that doubled me over, and a blow to my ribs that put me on the ground.

"Should I kill him?" the hairy one asked.

"It's your choice."

I ran bent over into the darkness. All at once, the earth disappeared from beneath my feet, and I was rolling and falling and rolling.

I remember seeing a faint light, and feeling pain from my toes to my hair. There was movement around me and noise, and I was afraid the robbers had found me. I opened my eyes wider, but slowly, and now I thought I was dreaming.

Kneeling over me was an Indian. A real Indian—not one of those white men with a wig like you see in cowboy movies, but an old man with dark, wrinkled skin and long braids with beads in them. I tried to sit up.

"Lay still," he said.

The sun was now bright in my eyes. Behind the man stood a couple of Indian boys wearing only shorts. They were looking at me with frowns on their faces.

"I got robbed and beat up," I said. My mouth hurt when I talked.

The man nodded. "You'll be all right." He turned to one of the boys. "Bring the horse."

The way I was hurting, I didn't see how I was going to be able to sit on a horse. A motor cranked, and the boy rode up on one of those four-wheelers. The boys got me standing and into a little cart behind the four-wheeler, and we headed out across the desert. My ribs hurt every time the thing bumped.

After a couple of miles of riding, we stopped at some gray cinder-block houses with a bunch of dogs barking out front. The old man and the boys put me on a cot in one of the houses, and one boy brought in a pan of water and some towels and washed the dried blood off my face. Another one brought me a big tin cup filled with cool water. My lip was busted and one eye felt swollen, and my knees were scraped.

"What's your name?" the old man asked me.

"Elbridge Snipes."

"I'm George Blackhawk. Do you hurt much?"

I pointed to my ribs. "I think one might be broken."

The old man left the room and returned with a leather

sack. "Lay very still," he said. From the sack he took out what looked like chicken bones and feathers and seeds, each one wrapped in some kind of paper. He unwrapped them and placed them at various spots on my chest and legs. "This will take the pain away."

I started getting nervous. I knew about black magic and that stuff, and how it was connected with the devil. I raised my arm to brush the mess off, but stopped it in midair. I didn't hurt anymore. My ribs had been throbbing, but all of a sudden they didn't hurt one bit. I let my arm drop.

"You a medicine man?" I asked.

"I'm a doctor."

I'd never seen a doctor that used bones, but I wasn't hurting now either. I said a quick prayer so that if this was black magic, God would protect me.

"You need to sleep," the old man said. He took another little package from his bag. Inside were what looked like dried leaves. "Chew this and swallow the juice," he told me, and held the leaves in front of my lips. The taste was bitter, but as I chewed, my tongue and lips got numb. Wasn't five minutes and I was out.

One of the Indian boys woke me by shaking my arm. I opened my eyes and saw a white woman, a little on the plump side, standing over me. The old man was taking the bones and feathers and seeds from my chest.

"How are you feeling?" the woman asked.

"I'm better now. I thought I had a busted rib."

"What happened to you?"

"Two men robbed me."

She pulled a chair over to the cot and sat down and unbuckled a leather bag. She was dressed in jeans and a flannel shirt with the sleeves rolled up to her elbows, and had brown hair pulled back in a ponytail. I figured she was in her thirties. She took a stethoscope and a blood pressure cuff from the bag.

"Can I have your name?" she asked.

"Yes, ma'am. Elbridge Snipes."

"I'm Kathy Kirby. Do you have any identification on you, Elbridge?"

I shook my head. "They took my wallet."

"Are you in any trouble with the law?"

"No. Not a bit. I was just hitchhiking, and two guys picked me up and robbed me."

She took my blood pressure, then listened to my chest and felt my ribs and head. "You may have a couple of cracked ribs, but I won't know without an X ray."

"I don't have any money."

"Money's not necessary. But you'll need to come with me to the clinic."

While she packed her gear, I thanked the old man. Then I went out with her to her jeep. "I'll try to drive easy," she said. "These roads are pretty rough."

"Are you from around here?" I asked her as we drove away.

"Gracious, no. I grew up in Atlanta." She told me her story: how she had gone to nursing school, then joined the Peace Corps and spent two years in some place with big mountains called Nepal, then worked in a hospital in Africa. She seemed eager to talk.

"I saw a lot of beauty, but I saw even more ugliness. There's too much sickness in the world. When I came back to the States, I tried a hospital in Atlanta. I couldn't stand all those walls, so I went to work for the Red Cross. I've been in this valley for three years."

I wanted to hear about that place Nepal. "Those mountains, were they near water?"

"No, they were quite a ways from water. Unless you count snow."

"A man told me there are some mountains near here that are close to water. I'm going there."

"You must mean the Cascades."

"That's them."

"Well, they're fairly near the ocean. Why do you need to go there?"

"I just need to. I'm not sure yet."

She turned and looked at me.

After about twenty minutes of dirt roads, we came to a little town. "Is this where the clinic is?" I asked.

"This is the big town of Kelly. There's a Catholic school here, and the clinic, and about five hundred Nez Percé."

I thought about the old man with his bones and feathers and seeds. "That old Indian gave me some leaves to chew. He said he was a doctor."

She smiled. "George is one of the oldest men on the reservation. In a way, he's a doctor. Did the leaves make you feel better?"

"Yeah. I went to sleep."

"George practices the old tribal medicine. It's what you believe. If you believe something, it'll usually work for you."

Wasn't much to the town, just a dusty main street and a bunch of cinder-block buildings. Kathy stopped in front of a whitewashed building at the end of the street. A large red cross was painted above the doors. Inside, the air smelled like Clorox. An Indian woman sat behind a desk.

"Hey, Jane," Kathy said. "Any catastrophes here while I was gone?"

"No. Billy One Bird came in with another knife wound. It wasn't bad. I cleaned it and put a couple of butterflies on it, and told him to come back tomorrow."

"Was he drinking again?"

"He was breathing, so I guess he was drinking."

Kathy sighed and shook her head, then led me into another room. "I want to get an X ray first. You need to take off your shirt."

I rolled my shoulders against the machine as I had learned to do in the hospital. Kathy had me turn a few ways. The machine hummed and clicked while she stood behind a screen.

"You can put your shirt back on. You act like you're a pro at X rays."

"I've had a few."

She sat me down, and thumped and poked and listened to my chest. When the pictures were ready, she held them against the window light. Then she put them on her desk and sat down in front of me.

"You have one cracked rib and a good bit of bruising and swelling."

"That man kicked me."

She paused a minute. "I see other things that concern me. Have you had an injury to your lungs? It looks like you have a considerable amount of scar tissue."

"I was in a fire. The doctor said I sucked the flames in."

"Was this recently? Will you tell me about it?"

I took a deep breath and started telling Kathy about that day. I told her about the doves flying good and about Rita and the girls and how I tried to knock down the door and go in that fire. I had to blink back tears. "I wanted to get to them, but God called them home. I wish he'd taken me too." I told her about being in the hospital and seeing people dying with tubes pushed down their throats. I told her about my vision and that I had to go over those mountains. "There's a reason for all this happening. I don't know what, but I believe there is one."

Her eyes were shiny when I stopped talking. "Well," she said, "you've had a rough time. I can't blame you for leaving the South."

"But I like it there. It's green, and doves coo in the morning. Still, I had to come here. There's a reason for it. If I didn't believe God made that fire for a reason, I'd go crazy."

Kathy wrapped my chest in bandages and tape. "This ought to make your ribs feel better for now. I'll give you some Tylenol for the pain. Mostly you have to rest. The worst thing that could happen is for you to get pneumonia."

"I've had my share of pneumonia. The doctor said next time it might kill me."

She picked up the phone and talked to someone for a few minutes. When she hung up, she looked at her hands. "I called the hospital in Grand Coulee. I'd like you to rest for a couple of days, but there aren't any beds until day after tomorrow." She paused. "I have an extra room at home. You can stay there a few days until the swelling goes down."

"I don't have any money to pay you."

"I don't want payment."

"I can cook for you. I cook real good."

*

Kathy's house was a little ways outside of town. It was bright blue with yellow trim. Flowers grew in the yard, and a wind chime tinkled from a tree limb.

"You got a pretty place," I told her.

"It's home. You should have seen it when I moved here. Gardening and reading are about the only things to do in this town. Unless you drink."

"I don't drink."

I spent two nights in her spare bedroom under clean sheets. The pain got better and the swelling went down. The first whole day I was there, while Kathy was doing her rounds, I sat in the sun and let it warm my sore muscles. That evening we sat at the picnic table in her backyard and ate supper while the sun dropped into the desert. She had a nice little garden back there, and some chickens in a pen. It reminded me of when me and Rita had lived at Turner's farm before the drought and fire.

"Do you believe in God?" I asked Kathy.

She didn't answer right away. "I don't think about it anymore."

"What you mean?"

Kathy told me about working in a relief camp in Africa and seeing little babies die with their bellies all swollen. "I quit praying and quit worrying about it." She waved her hand toward the sunset. "There's probably something out there that understands all of this. But I don't try to figure it out anymore. The hurt is too bad."

I rolled my tongue around, thinking for the words to tell her how wrong she was. The phone started ringing inside, and Kathy hurried to answer it. She came out grim-faced and said it was an emergency. Then she ran to her jeep and drove off, just as the sun blinked into the horizon.

*

I raised myself up in bed and saw on the clock that midnight had passed. Soft weeping was coming from the living room. "Kathy?" I called. The crying stopped. "Kathy, are you all right?"

I heard footsteps, and she appeared in the doorway. Her face was streaked with tears.

"What's wrong?"

She walked in and sat at the foot of the bed. "I'm sorry." She snorted and wiped her face with a Kleenex. "Billy One Bird hung himself. I tried everything to revive him." She covered her face with her hands.

"He was a friend of yours?"

She nodded. "He had a baseball scholarship to Washington State but quit after a year. When he came back here, he started drinking and getting in trouble. I tried my best to get him to return to school."

"I'm real sorry, Kathy."

She covered her face again. I wanted to do something to comfort her, so I put my hand on her shoulder. She leaned toward me with her face against mine. "I'm so terribly lonely here. People always sick or dying. Sometimes I don't think I can stand it any longer."

"You know they need you." I patted Kathy's shoulder, and she settled deeper against me, her face warm and wet. I could feel her breath. I put my arms around her, and she hugged me back. I had never hugged another woman besides Rita. When she started moving her lips against my neck, shivers went down my spine. I knew I should walk out of the room, but holding her felt so good. She unbuttoned my shirt and then her own, and pressed her bare chest against mine. Her heat was like medicine. "This is all right, Elbridge," she whispered. "This is a good thing." She put her lips to mine; I could taste salt. Then all I could see was Rita's face, and I heard the girls crying in that fire, and I pushed back from Kathy and ran out. I think now that was the bigger sin.

In the morning, I felt funny joining Kathy in the kitchen. We were both quiet, until finally she looked up from her coffee. "I'm sorry about last night. I shouldn't have done that."

"It wasn't you, Kathy. I just couldn't."

"You don't have to explain. I understand."

"I guess I'll be leaving today. I need to get over those mountains."

She smiled, but I think she was sad underneath. "It's different over those mountains," she said. "It rains a lot. The ocean brings in storms. The air is wet and chilly, even in the summer."

"I'll be okay. I been rained on."

"Elbridge, your lungs. They're in bad shape. The air here in the valley is dry and clean. But over there, it wouldn't be healthy for you. You could get pneumonia."

"I have to go. There's a reason for everything that happened to me. I have to go find out why."

She looked again into her cup. "I know that," she said softly. "I know you have to."

At the door, she handed me some folded bills. I told her I didn't need any money.

She stuck the money in my shirt pocket, then put a hand on each of my shoulders. "You have to eat. You need to keep dry. If you get a cold, you go straight to a public clinic. They'll treat you even if you're broke. They have to."

"I'll be fine."

"I don't know what it is you're looking for out there,

but I hope you find it." She held me tight for several seconds, then pushed away and planted a kiss on my cheek. "You better git. The mail truck leaves in ten minutes. It'll take you to Grand Coulee. You should be able to get a ride there. Don't get in any more cars. Just semis."

I lifted my bag and started walking. At the street corner I looked back at the house. Kathy stood framed in the doorway. I lifted my arm and saluted her; she waved, then closed the door.

That night, I slept on the banks of the Columbia River. At dawn I hitched a ride in a logging truck. The cab smelled of tobacco and coffee. "You going over the mountains, sir?" I asked the driver.

"Just up to where they're cutting. That's almost to the pass. Over the pass, it's all downhill to Seattle."

The truck grunted its way up through a bunch of switchbacks, never getting above third gear. I saw patches of slushy ice, and my ears were popping. After about an hour, there were big tracts of land where the forest had been cut clear.

At one spot the driver braked and turned into a muddy side road. "I hate to put you out in the middle of the woods, buddy," he said, "but this is my stop. The pass is only a couple of miles up the road. There'll be a lot of trucks heading down toward Seattle this afternoon."

I thanked him and climbed out of the truck. The air was cool and moist, the sun real bright. I started up the grade and in no time was breathing heavy; I had to stop often to rest. Around a curve, the road straightened out and went to a point against the sky. I sucked down air and kept walking, the sky getting bigger and bigger. At last, the road leveled, and what I saw took my breath. The mountains rolled down into hills, and beyond the hills was water so blue it hurt my eyes. The water spread to the horizon, where it joined up with the sky; I felt like I was looking into eternity. Right in the middle of the road, I dropped to my knees.

Lewis

I'VE BEEN LOOKING at the moon and trying to see the face that's supposed to be in it. I never could see a face there, not even when I was a child. Maybe I don't want to see it. Maybe I don't like the idea of a face that watches over the whole earth, so I just see light there and some dark places that are supposed to be dried-up seas. I don't like pretending anyway. I know now how easy it is for a man to look at a person or a dog or anything and see just what he needs to see. I was swallowed up in a big city, and every day hundreds of people looked right through me or around me, but not at me. Sitting here in the cold, holding Elbridge, I feel the most communion with people that I have felt in a year. A man doesn't have to see ugliness. Not if he has a few dollars to spare.

The grid of streets surrounding Pioneer Square was filling with cars and pedestrians by the time Lewis returned. He'd walked ten blocks to find a church he hadn't already visited.

After months of wandering, Lewis had finally found a sense of peace within this park. Pioneer Square offered him the shade of large trees and grassy areas with benches to sit on; there were also a few gazebos, a large fountain, and several modern sculptures scattered about. The park was bordered by shops and restaurants, beyond which rose steel-and-glass skyscrapers. If he looked west, he could see several miles of bay, stopped by the rugged Olympic Mountains; if he looked east, the valley's gradual rise to the wall of the Cascades. Home was in the center of the park, a mattress of folded cardboard under a large oak; on rainy nights he slept in a Salvation Army clothes bin on a sidewalk near the park.

As Lewis approached, he saw a man sitting on his bed. He shouted, and the man stood and staggered away. Lewis lowered his duffel bag, sat down on the cardboard, and pulled out a bottle of Popov. He poured a few inches into a tin cup, then gulped the liquor down. He lay back and looked through the tree branches into the sky. Like a bowl in a bowl, he thought. I'm like a worm inside a double cocoon, 'cept I'm not coming out of this as a butterfly.

The sun was warm on his face. Summer was mild in Seattle, but winter came early, Lewis had heard, with cold rain and snow. Soon the ice would slide in like a glacier, and for months it would cover the grass in the park. Ice and flesh didn't mix too well, and Lewis thought of the mastodon, buried by the ice, its bones given back to the earth. For now, this was his place, where memories, his old world and life, were held back by the miles and by walls of granite and concrete and steel. At night, tucked inside his sleeping bag, vodka in his belly, he would stare at a spot of sky and imagine himself hurtling deeper and deeper into space so no eye on earth could see him. His medicine would keep his mind blank, and he could end it as soon as the man upstairs got tired of the game.

Scattered about Pioneer Square were various bums and drunks and weirdos. Young men with tattered backpacks and long hair and beards; old drunks sleeping wherever their bottles felled them, curled with their jugs tucked against their bellies; assorted crazies babbling to themselves. Lewis had never seen such a concentrated display of the homeless and shiftless and pitiful, but he understood why they congregated there. Within a few blocks were liquor stores, inside an easy walk were homeless shelters. From almost any trashcan in the park you could fish out half-eaten sandwiches and paper cups with something left in the bottom.

The people only passing through or around the park seemed comfortable, purposeful, with stable lives and jobs. They were mostly well dressed and neatly groomed, young to middle-aged. If they even looked at Lewis and his neighbors, it was only for a second, after which, eyes forward, they marched toward their destinations. While they might occasionally flip a quarter into a soup can or an open guitar case, they did not communicate with the panhandler or music man, the wino or babbling idiot. Lewis felt like a ghost passing among them; they apparently crossed him out of their world. Perhaps they, unlike the horde who came to gawk at him at the freak show, did not need to be cleansed.

Lewis poured himself another shot and drained it. He pulled a box of Cracker Jack from his bag, ate a handful or two, then threw some of the peanuts to a squirrel. Several yards from him stood an old mongrel dog, his head down, rear end twitching. One of his hind legs was only a stump, and his ribs showed through his skin; most of the dog's hair was lost to mange. "You 'bout as fucked up as me," Lewis said. He reached back into his bag and brought out half of a loaf of bread and some bologna, then tossed a few slices of bread and meat to the dog. Keeping his eyes on Lewis, the mongrel stepped tentatively toward the food, gulped it down, and hurried away with his three-legged gait. Lewis looked at a digital clock on the side of a building, and saw it was time to go. He rose heavily to his feet, shouldered his bag, and headed toward the market.

Pike Place Market lay several blocks from the park at the bottom of a steep hill, its open-air shops and stalls attracting crowds. Produce was stacked in neat piles, all of it fresh and gleaming. Fishmongers stood behind mounds of salmon and tuna, oysters and clams, shouting the daily specials; the smell was salty and pungent. Butchers hoisted big sides of beef and cut steaks to order on thick wooden blocks. Craft vendors displayed tie-dyed T-shirts, pottery, and jewelry.

Stationed here and there in the market were performers and beggars—a man playing bad banjo, his open instrument case sprinkled with a few coins; two black men singing a cappella; a young woman who would read palms for a dollar; a juggler; a man with dark glasses and a cane and a plastic cup.

Lewis continued the length of the market and went to sit on a strip of grass in the sun, his back against a low brick wall. He took a drink of vodka, then searched in his duffel; out came an old cigar box, which he placed between his feet. He felt the warm sun on his face; the liquor was working.

A woman walked by and, without looking directly at Lewis, stooped and dropped a dollar bill in the cigar box. Lewis's eye closed. When he awoke an hour later, the box held some coins and a few bills. He was in a crazy world, he thought, where no one saw him and money fell from the sky.

Elbridge

I'M TIED TO THIS EARTH with only a thread. Not even that—a strand of spider web. I feel like a kite in March, wanting to climb higher and higher into the sky and held back by just a string. I ain't far from flying. The stars seem so low now, almost floating around my ears. I see people in the sky, millions of them, moving in and out of each other like a person working his fingers together, and I hear voices and music and singing and clapping like someone turned a radio on. I want to go in there with them, but this string is holding me down. I think it'll let go soon, and I'll be free.

Lewis saved me. They were fixing to put a tube down my throat. There in the hospital, I wouldn't have been able to see the moon and the stars coming down to take me. I wish there was something I could do for him. He talks to me, pulls that blanket up around my body. I never saw more pain in a man. I thought I knew pain, but Lewis hurts from his scars to his soul. I wish I could help him, but a man has to help himself. I know that now better than I know my name. You can't wait for salvation to come down from the clouds. You got to pull it from inside you. You can't stay locked inside the temple waiting for someone to bring you the key. That key is in your own hand. I've been on a journey and crossed walls that rose into the clouds. But you can't let walls hold you. If there ain't a door in that wall, then make one.

The sun was low when I hit the Seattle city limits, and the skyline was glowing. I got out of the semi that brought me and started walking, with my eye on this real tall building that glittered like gold. My stomach was queasy, 'cause I knew this was where I was meant to come to, and the answer was here.

It was dark when I got downtown, which was full of tall buildings. I turned a corner, and there in the middle of all that brick and steel and asphalt was a small piece of woods. There was a path leading into the trees, and over it was a sign that said "Pioneer Square."

Some rough-looking guys were standing under a street-lamp. "Hey, buddy, come here," one of them said to me. I kept walking. I'd learned a lot about the nature of some people. A little farther along, I saw a woman sitting on a bench. When I got even with her, she lifted her sweater and showed me her breasts. I shifted my eyes forward and kept walking. I left the sidewalk and went into the darkness of the trees. My feet hurt, and my belly was gnawing with hunger, and I wanted to sit down. I had nearly reached the trunk of a big tree when I heard a voice.

"This is my spot."

I stopped and peered into the shadows; my eyes still

weren't used to the dark. Slowly I made out the shape of a man. He was sitting against the tree trunk, and a cigarette was glowing at what must have been his mouth.

"I'm sorry," I said. He didn't answer, but his cigarette glowed brighter. In a way, I felt better in the dark; it made everyone equal. "You know a cheap place around here to eat?"

"You can eat free out of the trashcans. There's a Burger King on the north side of the park if you're particular."

I had an urge to see the man's face. "Go on now," he said. "I don't keep company."

I took a step backward. "Is it safe to sleep in here?"

The man chuckled, but he sounded bitter. "That depends on how damn mean and ugly you are."

I knew to leave him then.

At Burger King, I bought two hamburgers and a small fries. I sat in a booth and stared into the lights outside and thought about the man under the tree. I had felt drawn to him, as if his cigarette was a signal.

I chewed slow and wondered where I might get work here. The money Kathy had given me was going fast. Maybe I could wash dishes or something. I knew how to cook breakfast good. I stayed in my seat until some of the weariness had washed from my legs, then cleared the table and went back out.

In the park, I chose a place near a lamppost, where there was no one else. If someone was going to try and rob me again, I wanted to be able to see 'em and have a swinging chance. I spread my blanket and rolled up in it, and used my bag as a pillow. The air was chilly.

Dear God, I began to pray, then stopped. The words weren't there. I closed my eyes and slept.

Sometime probably after midnight, the rain moved in. When I woke up, I was soaked through to my clothes. I tried to ignore the water for a while, but it got harder, so I packed up and went to a bus shelter beside the street. That helped me quit shivering a little. I dozed off and on through the night, until I opened my eyes and saw a gray, wet morning.

I cleared my throat a couple of times and breathed in deeply. That feeling was there in my lung, and I couldn't deny it—a deep, itchy pain that always came before the coughing.

Lewis

A STEADY RAIN drummed against the top of the Salvation Army bin. Lewis lay warm and dry on the bed of discarded clothing, his first drink of the day beginning to numb that little spot in the middle of his forehead. Several shots were left in the bottle, and he was content to wait out the rain. Usually it quit by midmorning.

He had moved from under the tree the night before, as soon as the first splats of rain hit his face. When he got to the bin, he found two men inside; he told them to leave, and they went away without an argument. A few times during the night he had heard someone pulling on the door, but to no avail; as always, he had secured it with a piece of wire.

The dance on the metal roof eventually ended, and Lewis finished off his vodka and buried the bottle under the clothes. He untwisted the wire and put it in his pocket, and slid open the door. He checked for policemen on the street, which was already crowded with people, then hauled himself out. At a corner hot-cart he stopped for his usual breakfast. The vendor nodded and took a pretzel from the warmer, smeared it with mustard, and handed it to him, along with a bottle of orange juice. Lewis gave him two dollars. He wolfed down the pretzel and emptied the bottle of juice. Now, with what remained of yesterday's earnings in his pocket, he would make his daily visit to the liquor store, five blocks from the park in a shabby residential area. It was the same route every day, in front of the same run-down houses. Today the path in front of one house was blocked by a pickup truck parked on the sidewalk; two men were moving furniture into the house. Children played in the small dirt yard, and one of them, a boy of about five wearing only a pair of dirty shorts, stared at Lewis as he passed.

"Heh-wo," he said, raising his hand.

Lewis swung his head toward the child. Scabs and grime marked his face and neck, and he had a harelip.

"Heh-wo," the boy repeated, still staring.

Lewis nodded and walked on. Few people had looked into his face and spoken to him since he'd left the carnival.

On his way back from the liquor store, Lewis saw the harelipped boy again. He looked up from where he was drawing in the dirt, and stood and walked toward Lewis.

"You got burned," the boy said.

Lewis stopped and studied him.

"What's your name?" the boy asked.

Lewis hesitated a moment, then said his name.

"Heh-wo, Wuwis."

One of the men moving furniture approached from behind the truck. His eyes narrowed, and he hurried over and grabbed the boy by one arm.

"Get in the yard, you little shit," he yelled, dragging the boy and pushing him into the dirt. The boy began crying. Lewis smothered the sound with his footsteps, as he headed for the market to receive the day's offering.

By noontime, Lewis was deep in his bottle, his mind somewhere in the realms of the universe. A familiar sound pulled him to earth.

"God loves you," a voice proclaimed. "He'll be with you when no one else is."

Lewis had heard plenty of voices like this before, but try as he might, he couldn't shut it off. Yeah, God loves me, Lewis thought. All those quarters he drops into my box. Got me living like a king. Yeah, that cocksucker loves me.

He searched for the source of the voice. Atop a low wall across the street stood a short, skinny man with carrot-red hair and bright blue eyes. He held one hand out above his head as he shouted. About a dozen people were gathered in front to listen.

Yeah, he's got his scam, Lewis thought. He'll be passing the collection plate to raise a little money so he can do God's work. Soon as he gets a couple of dollars, he'll have to go get himself a jug of wine and start having Communion. At least he's original—this is the first preaching I've heard down here.

The man leaned forward and began coughing violently. As his listeners dispersed, he bent over with spasms. Finally he stepped down from the wall, his face red, his body heaving.

Them cigarettes killing you, Jack, Lewis thought.

Marijuana, whatever it is. You better get to the punch line a little faster, get the hat circulating. People are moved by the Word just so long.

The little man stopped coughing. He wiped his mouth with his hand and disappeared down the street. Lewis closed his eye and turned the world off.

Elbridge

I LAID DOWN in some grass and rested, took deep breaths and tried not to cough. I was shocked, not by the coughing—I knew it was coming sooner or later—but that I had stood up and talked to people.

The itch in my lungs was like a weed growing. I couldn't hold it back any longer, and the first cough was like a dam breaking. I rolled onto my belly and spat up what was inside me. When I could stand, I went to the street and found a policeman, and he told me where a free hospital was.

The Friends' Hospital was on a ridge west of downtown; it was an old brick building two stories high. I had to wait nearly an hour before the doctor saw me. He took X rays and listened to me with his stethoscope and thumped me while I told him my story.

When I was finished, he told me Seattle was about the worst place I could be with my condition. "You need to be in a place like Arizona, where the air is very dry."

"I need to be here, Doctor. I come a long way."

"I can get you a bus ticket back to your home through

Social Services. You must still have some family there?"

"None that matters."

"Your lungs are in bad shape. Another infection could kill you. I have to be frank. I don't think you'll last the winter on the streets here."

I looked through the window toward the mountains I had come over. "I got to stay here, Doctor. There's a reason for it."

"Let me admit you for the night. We'll run some IV antibiotics through you. They work faster."

I nodded. "Okay."

The next day at noon I left the hospital, carrying a sack of pills. I couldn't hitch a ride and ended up walking the couple of miles back to Pioneer Square. Most of the trip was downhill, so walking was easy, but I breathed in a lot of car fumes. I had to stop a few times for coughing fits and reached the park in the afternoon. I rested on a bench for an hour and ate some of them pills and counted my money—twelve dollars and some change. I needed work. I started toward the market.

At the end of this one street, Pike Place, was a low brick wall with a good view of the bay. It pulled me strong as a magnet as I walked through the market. Words began forming in my head, words I couldn't turn off— it was like I had a record playing inside my head. I wanted to go hide somewhere, but that wall kept pulling me, until I stepped up on it and the words started coming out.

"Y'all see those mountains out there," I shouted. "Y'all know who lives in them mountains?"

A few people stopped and stared at me. I swallowed hard and kept yelling. "God lives in those mountains.

You see that big blue water out there? God lives in that water too. I used to think He just lived in church. But now I know that ain't right."

Several more people stopped to listen, and the words were coming so fast I had to spit them out. "You know something else? Names don't really matter. You take a rock. You can call it a boulder or a stone or a pebble or a grain of sand, but it's still rock. Names don't matter. I've come to learn that. That's something I know."

I felt light-headed, and my eyes misted over. The faces and bodies of the people in front of me jumbled together. I told them about the mountains and rivers I'd seen, about laying in the desert and really seeing the stars.

"I used to think the Lord lived in church, but now I know He was just trapped in there. The temple is a prison if you keep the door locked."

The words left me as suddenly as they had filled me. "I don't have any more to say," I told the folks who had been listening. They mumbled as they broke apart and some of them threw change on the ground. "I wasn't asking for money," I said, but that didn't hold them back. I hadn't begged for that money. I wasn't ashamed. It was the Lord providing. I picked it up and counted more than three dollars.

When my heart had slowed down enough, I stuffed the money in my pocket and started up Pike Place. Something made me stop in my tracks and take a deep breath. I saw a big man sitting close to a wall, leaning against a duffel bag. His head was tipped back, and he was asleep. Between his legs was a little box with coins and dollar bills in it. He must have been in a fire sometime; half his face was like melted wax. It hurt to look at him, and a shiver crossed me. I dug some change from my pocket and dropped it in his box.

Lewis

SHOPPERS WERE EXITING the market when Lewis awoke. He collected his money and put it in his pocket, then stood and walked toward Pioneer Square. He debated whether he should go to the homeless shelter, where he could have a hot meal and a shower. He thought of the long line he would find there, all those other broken and defeated people. No, he didn't need a shower after all, and right now he could stop at a deli for some hot dogs and bread.

Back at his cardboard mattress, Lewis unpacked for the night. He pulled his bottle and tin cup from his duffel, then his flashlight and a musty sleeping bag. After pouring himself a drink and downing it, he tore open a loaf of bread and folded a slice around a hot dog. The sandwich was gone in three bites, and he ate another just as quickly.

In the twilight, Lewis could see the old mongrel dog approaching, limping worse than usual. "Hey, boy," Lewis called. "Somebody kick you? You got to learn to use your teeth." The dog wagged his tail. Lewis slung out a hot dog and several slices of bread, and the animal hurried for the meal.

Lewis spread his sleeping bag and lay down. A breeze stirred the tree boughs, and what sky he could see was cloud-covered. The world was shrinking on him, the mountains on the horizon sliding closer and higher, the skyscrapers curling in like great waves.

Lewis heard the rustle of leaves, the sound of steps. He lifted his head and saw the shape of a man a few yards away. "This spot is claimed," he growled.

The man shuffled closer; he coughed twice into his hand. "My name is Elbridge."

"So what?"

"You went into a fire, didn't you?"

Lewis pulled up on one elbow. He knew that voice.

"You went right into that fire, didn't you?" the man repeated. He coughed again, softly.

Now Lewis remembered—the little man on the wall, with the preaching scam. "Look, fellow, I don't know nothing about any fire. I do know I want you to get the hell away from me right now. Understand?"

"You know . . . you know that God cares about you?"

Lewis grabbed a handful of acorns from the ground and threw them. "You and God go stroll across that bay, preacher man. You better start right now."

The man turned and walked into the night.

As the days slipped by, Lewis continued with his usual routine. In the mornings he made his run to the liquor store, then nodded through most of the remaining hours. The warmth of summer had passed; darkness came earlier, and clouds were more frequent.

On this afternoon, one like many another, Lewis collected his offering at the market. He could have sworn he'd seen a ten-dollar bill in his box at one point, but when he counted, he came up with only five singles and a few bucks in change. He started for Pioneer Square, his head throbbing and his stomach sour. He knew he needed food, but this money was for tomorrow's medication, two fifths required every day now. Lewis walked to a trash barrel on the corner, thrust his arm inside, and felt around. Half a hamburger wrapped in paper, some greasy onion rings stuck together, pieces of soft pretzel with teeth marks in them, a whole candied apple—he uncrumpled a paper sack and dropped the scraps of food inside.

Lewis trudged across the street into the park, passing the preaching man, who sat on a bench, wrapped tightly in a blanket. The man's head went up and he said hello, but Lewis did not answer. He felt the man's eyes burning in his back. Let him look as much as he wants, Lewis thought; plenty others have.

Lewis settled into his spot, feeling the chill in the air. He needed two hefty drinks for the numbness to set in. Frost would begin to roll down from the mountains in a few weeks; and he would let it cover him like a blanket, and in those cold wraps would find rest.

A Monday morning, and Lewis was slow getting out of his sleeping bag. His pulse was heavy in his ears. He had finished his vodka Saturday night and on Sunday had had to drink fortified wine to get to the neutral zone. He counted his money—barely enough—then set off for the liquor store. After a block, his head was spinning; he stopped and held on to a lamp pole. A drink would straighten things out. Five blocks and he'd be all right.

Lewis neared the house where the harelipped boy lived. He hadn't seen the kid outside lately, but this morning he was there, playing on the porch with one of his sisters. The kid raised his arm to wave, then flashed his head toward the house as if he was fearful of someone watching. Lewis marched on to the store.

He got his bottles and counted out change and crumpled bills into the clerk's hand. Once outside the store, he slumped against the wall, unscrewed the cap on one bottle, and drank from it. He closed his eye and felt the liquor burn its way down his raw gullet, and collect like a puddle of fire in his belly. After about a minute, he felt the good crawl of alcohol on his forehead. When the dizziness had slowly leached from him, he took another dose and started for Pike Place, where money fell from the sky.

This time when he passed the harelipped boy's house, the child's father sat on the front porch, a beer in one hand, a cigarette in the other. Some children played behind him.

"A fucking freak," the man said.

Lewis kept walking. He did not turn to look.

"Hey, shithead," the man told his son. "See that freak? He's uglier than you. About the only thing uglier."

Lewis kept walking. The liquor was strong in his blood, and a veil was closing around him, shutting out the world.

Elbridge

MY COUGHING got worse by the day. I doubled up on the antibiotics, tried to eat good and stay warm. I thought about going back to the Friends' Hospital but already knew they'd say I needed to be in a bed. What I had come all this way for was between the park and that wall at the end of Pike Place. I'd felt it as soon as I got over that last range of mountains, and the knowledge grew in me like the itch in my lungs.

I had just finished speaking at Pike Place and was on my way back to the park when I passed by the burned man again. He was half asleep, as usual. I was right in front of him when a man stooped and took a handful of money from his box.

"Hey," I shouted. "That's his money."

The guy was in his early twenties, about my age. He looked cheap.

"That's his money," I said. "You're stealing."

The guy squinted at me. "Who the fuck are you, the police?"

"You shouldn't steal."

He came over and hit me hard on the face. For a second I saw red and curled my fists. But like a bolt of lightning had struck me, I remembered hitting Rita that night just before she died, and then what Kathy said when we were driving to the clinic: *There's too much sickness in the world.* I took a deep breath and just stood there. "You can hit me again, but I ain't fighting. If you take his money, I'll yell. There's a policeman on the corner."

The guy shifted his eyes. "You ain't worth skinning my knuckles," he said. He dropped the money in the box and walked away.

I kneeled and shook the burned man's shoulder. "Put your money away. Folks will steal it."

He pulled his head back and opened his eye.

"Put your money in your pocket," I told him again. "People will steal it."

His eye closed and his head flopped. I picked up the bills from his box and stuffed them in his pocket. My cheek hurt from where that guy had hit me. For the first time in my life, I hadn't fought back; but I didn't feel whipped. For the first time in my life, I understood what turning the other cheek meant.

Lewis

LEWIS FADED IN AND OUT of consciousness all day. At twilight he pulled himself standing. He was alarmed to see only a few coins in his box, but then he felt a wad of bills in his shirt pocket. He held to the wall until his head stopped spinning. His belly ached as if it were filled with nails; his temples throbbed. Lewis tipped his bottle, put it in his bag, then went up the street toward Pioneer Square.

A cool wind was coming off the bay, a dark line of clouds rolling in from the ocean. Lewis pawed through a trashcan, found a half-gnawed chicken leg and a tuna sandwich with only one bite taken from it. He lifted his head and gazed at the storm, sweeping inland like an airborne tidal wave. He looked back at the bite mark in the sandwich and dropped the food into the trashcan.

At the park, he took his sleeping bag and weaved his way to where several men sat around a fire of wood scraps. He stood above them, and they looked at him without speaking.

Lewis tossed the sleeping bag to the ground. "Winner take all. It's a battle royal."

Back at his cardboard, he pulled the remaining fifth from his duffel. "Me and you got a little date, bottle. Yeah, me and you are buddies."

He drank until he had to stop for air. "Let's call it even," he shouted into the sky. "I didn't quit, and you damn sure didn't let up any either. Let's end this thing tonight."

A raindrop splatted against his head. Lewis turned the bottle up again, the liquor like lava in his throat. He settled on the cardboard and closed his eye, his body seeming to turn, as if he lay in a great whirlpool. The universe raced around and around him, ever tighter and faster. The cold rain, first falling in fat, slow drops, became a sharp downpour. Lewis drew himself into fetal position as the rain hammered against him. He sucked what was left of his liquor; the mouth of the bottle fit his own as neatly as might the barrel of a gun.

Phoenix

THE NIGHT TURNED SLOWLY, and Orion with his sword loomed like a guard above the two men. As the moon sank into the western sky, Venus topped the mountains, a fiery eye in the clear, thin air, walking vanguard for the sun.

Lewis

I SEE THE MORNING STAR climbing over those rocks, and have never welcomed it more. The sun is probably only a couple of hours away. Elbridge seems lighter and lighter in my arms; he's leaking away in the night. Sometimes I whisper in his ear for him to keep holding on, that the birds are coming.

Maybe I'm getting as crazy as him, but I swear sometimes I feel arms around me. I'll be shivering, and suddenly this warmth will come over me like someone's hugging me. I don't reckon I'm freezing to death. They say a person gets warm when he's close to freezing. But

I can still think, and they also say a man's thoughts get addled when he's freezing. I know I have to keep my mind right and stay awake till the sun rises. I don't expect a St. Bernard to come up here with a little keg of brandy and a couple of blankets and save us.

I've been thinking of that word—salvation. Elbridge used to always talk about salvation. You can pull a man from a lake a dozen times, but if he doesn't want to be saved, he'll keep jumping back in the water. People can reach out to you forever; but nothing comes of it unless you want to reach back to them.

"Drink it, man." Elbridge held a cup to Lewis's mouth, pressing the rim gently against his lower lip. "You need it, man. Drink it."

Lewis felt the plastic hard against his mouth, smelled the warm vapor. His mind returned from rain and crashing mountains. He opened his eye.

Gone were the big trees on Pioneer Square, the sky and the gateway to eternity. Instead, Lewis saw the preaching man above him.

"Get the fuck out of my face!" Lewis warned.

"You need to drink this. It'll warm you up."

"I don't need to be fucking warm. I died last night."

The little man stirred the cup with his finger, which he then licked clean. "You come close to it. You ought to eat this soup. It's cream of mushroom."

Lewis pushed himself up on one elbow. "Where the hell am I?"

"The Friends' Hospital. I found you sick and called an ambulance."

Lewis looked around the large room, which smelled strongly of disinfectant. He was in a ward filled with metal gurneys. He felt suddenly dizzy and put his head down against the pillow.

"You still got a fever," Elbridge said. "The doctor will be around in an hour or so."

"Why'd you have to bring me here? Why you always bugging me?" He recalled the stars blinking out, how he had felt the weight of steel and rock burying him. He had been close.

"You ought to drink this. You need some food."

Lewis slapped the cup from the man's hand, spilling soup across the floor. "Get the *hell* away from me," he said.

Elbridge stumbled backward. He took a deep breath and went to lie down on a bed across the aisle. He retched, then spit, into a plastic tub. Other patients in the ward sat up to look.

Lewis's head still spun, and he was shivering. How long had he been here, and where had his bottle gotten to? A nurse came and put a needle in his arm, and soon his eye fell shut.

Lewis was kept sedated much of the day; he was X-rayed, prodded, poked with needles. He spoke only when asked questions, and swallowed every pill he was given.

"You don't sound like you're from California," the young doctor told him.

"Well, I am."

"And you were burned in a car accident?"

"That's right."

The doctor studied the papers in his hand. "Well, I think we can knock out your pneumonia pretty easily. What concerns me is your alcohol consumption. Your liver is enlarged."

"Can that kill me?"

"Liver failure could."

"When can I get out of here?"

"Right now if you want to. I can't hold you." The doctor pointed toward the curtainless window. "It's raining out there. I wish you'd stay until we knock out your fever."

Liver failure, Lewis thought. That'll take you out. I need to walk to get liquor, and right now I ain't much for walking. "Pump it to me, Doc. I don't even feel pain anymore."

Lewis's fever broke that night, and he sweated his sheets wet, draining the poisons within him. The nurses injected him with tranquilizers to keep him from having withdrawal seizures, and he floated in the haze of the drugs.

Lewis woke to the smell of food. He opened his eye and saw a tray on a metal table beside his bed. Behind it stood the preaching man.

"Your breakfast is here. You ought to eat while it's hot."

"What are you? The damn cook or something?"

"I'm helping 'em serve. These eggs ain't bad when they're hot."

Lewis hadn't eaten since he'd been on the street. He sat up and peered at the food on the tray—a mound of scrambled eggs, a sausage patty, two slices of toast. He reached for what he assumed was coffee.

"It's decaf, but it's warm," the preacher said. "It feels good going down."

Lewis swallowed a mouthful of the tepid liquid. The man watched him intently. "Why the hell you always staring at me? Most people look the other way."

The man blinked rapidly and stuck out his hand. "I'm Elbridge Snipes. I'm glad to meet you, Lewis."

"How do you know my name?"

"It's on your chart."

Lewis hesitated before reaching out his claw hand and grasping the man's fingers.

"You went in that fire, didn't you? You saved somebody."

"You don't know a damn thing about me, man. Get the hell out of here."

Elbridge took a step backward, and his eyes welled with tears. "I tried to go in the fire too. I tried to go in there after them, but the fire was too hot. I tried to, but . . ." He began wheezing and coughing, his face contorted with pain.

When he went down on one knee, a nurse hurried over from across the ward. "Get the oxygen," she called to an orderly.

Lewis stared as the man fell against the floor; his skin had the pallor of lard.

At midmorning, the doctor made his rounds with the duty nurse. He paused and read the chart at Elbridge's bed. "Another attack?" he asked the nurse.

"The third in two days."

"Try to keep him comfortable." The doctor crossed the aisle to Lewis's bed. "How are you feeling this morning, Mr. Calhoon?"

"I'm breathing."

"I see your fever has broken. I think in a week or so we can get your liver counts stabilized."

"What if I was to drink now, Doc?" Lewis asked. "What if I walked out of here and got me a couple of fifths of vodka?"

"Well, right now a fifth of vodka would be suicide. It would be the same as putting a loaded gun to your head."

Lewis nodded. His mind swam back in time, to the image of a man kneeling on the edge of a river with a rifle in his hands. He remembered what the man had understood in those seconds, and his stomach twisted.

Leaning against the railing of the balcony, Lewis looked east. His eye fixed upon the great gray-and-white wall of the Cascades and Rainier.

That mountain just drifts there, Lewis thought, like some damn blocker on the offensive line: big and round, and nothing can go over it; even the airplanes have to fly around the sides. Snow covered the top of the mountain, and deer and bear were on the upper slopes now; they would migrate lower as the winter came. If a man tried to walk over that mountain, Lewis figured, he'd probably die.

The doctor had likened a bottle of liquor to a loaded gun. So death would still be by Lewis's own hand, and his passing would be just another sin.

I could start walking up that mountain, and the snows will swallow me, he reasoned. In the spring some bear will eat my carcass, and be glad for the meal and not judge me by how I died. It would be just as natural as breathing.

When Lewis awoke one morning from under a blanket of sedatives, it was to see a parade of drunks, street people, and other destitutes filing in and out of the ward. With their DTs, fight wounds, and bad livers, they reminded him of the life outside.

And there was another reminder. On his way to the

bathroom, he heard a voice he'd heard before. He halted at the doorway to the television room and looked in. There at the front of the room was Elbridge, with a handful of fellow patients seated before him.

At the sight of Lewis, Elbridge stopped preaching. "Come and join us," he said.

"Join what?"

"We're having services."

Lewis stared at the collection of worshippers, most of them maimed in some visible way, all of them maimed internally.

"We're giving thanks," Elbridge said. "We'd sure like you to join us."

"What in the hell do y'all have to give thanks about? Look at yourselves."

"We're alive. We have a day of life before us."

"Yeah." Lewis's voice was heavy with disgust. "We're alive. Ain't that just fucking peachy." He proceeded to the bathroom, then returned to the ward. And there, from his bed, he could still hear the drone of the preaching man.

Lewis was in bed skimming through a two-year-old *Reader's Digest* when he felt someone's presence. He turned to his left to see Elbridge.

"You mind if I talk to you, Lewis?"

"Yeah. I don't have nothing to talk about." He continued to hear the little man's labored breathing.

"It's a pretty day outside. The rain has stopped."

Lewis stared into his magazine.

"You're a brave man."

Lewis slapped the magazine closed. "Why do you keep bugging me?"

As if invited, Elbridge pulled a chair close to the bed and sat down. He looked directly into Lewis's eye. "You came close to it, didn't you?"

"Close to what?"

"Dying. You musta come close."

Lewis stared at the man, amazed at his talk. No one else really spoke to him; everyone talked through him or around him.

"I'm going to die soon," Elbridge said. "The doctor told me. I ain't scared, though. I'll get to see my wife and my girls then."

"You look healthy enough to me," Lewis told him.

"It's my lungs. They're all burned up." He coughed gently. "You went right in that fire, didn't you, Lewis?"

Lewis lifted himself to a sitting position. "I want you to tell me, man. What is this shit about fire?"

Elbridge was silent, then spoke slowly, each word measured by pain. "I tried to go in there. I could hear Cindy and Connie crying and that fire popping, and I was banging against the door and hitting it. I ain't big like you. I woulda gone right in the middle of it if I coulda busted that door." He sobbed into his hands.

Lewis wondered if the man was insane. He opened his mouth several times before he let the words go. "Your family burned up?"

"Rita and my two girls. She was going to have another baby." Elbridge tried to hold back the tears, and wiped his glistening cheeks. "If I was as big as you, I'd have gone right through that door, even if I burned clean up."

A cold rage swelled inside Lewis. "And you're glad you're alive? Your family burned up, and your lungs are shot, and you come here and tell me what a pretty day it is?"

"I'm waiting for a message. It ain't come yet."

The man's brain was as scorched as his lungs, Lewis thought. "The message is that you got fucked, mister."

Elbridge shook his head vigorously. "There was a reason for that fire. God don't do nothing without a reason. He just ain't told me why yet."

"Yeah, it's all for a reason. You play by his rules or you're out. Dead out."

"That fire was for the good. I'm just trying to keep living till I find out why."

Lewis pointed his stubbed hand toward his face. "This look like the good to you? You really looked at me?"

"I been looking at you since I got here. You're alive. You should be thankful."

Lewis threw his magazine across the room. "I didn't deserve this face. I didn't deserve any of what happened to me."

"It was for a reason, Lewis. One day you'll know why."

"Get away from me, man!" Lewis bellowed. "Get the hell back from me and take your unjust God with you!" Rage coursed through him like a swollen river, yet in the midst of his anger, he realized he could not remember how long it had been since he had felt such strong emotions.

After lunch, Lewis went to the balcony. In the parking lot below, a man pulled a garbage can filled with kitchen scraps to a dumpster. After emptying the can, he struck it against the ground and turned it upside down, leaving a residue of food in a circle.

The man had barely entered a door to the hospital kitchen when at least a dozen rats sprang from beneath the dumpster. Lewis could hear their squeals as they fought over the food. He could think only of his meals out of the garbage cans around Pioneer Square.

Lewis saw a shadow, a small spot of darkness moving across the ground. The rats must have seen it as well, for they stopped their fighting and squealed and hunkered close to the ground. Then, like a bolt of lightning, a hawk plunged claws-first into the mass of bodies. The huge bird skewered a rat in its talons, shrieked, and flapped its wings and lifted into the air, carrying aloft the struggling rodent. Lewis watched the hawk fly above the roofline and disappear. On the ground below, the rats resumed eating until the last morsel was devoured.

Lewis heard the door to the balcony open behind him. Who would be seeking his company? He didn't bother to turn around.

It was Elbridge who walked up beside him and looked toward the dumpster. "You saw the hawk, didn't you?"

Lewis nodded.

"It's the same every day," Elbridge said. "The man brings the slop out, then the rats come out, and then the hawk swoops down. It's always the same." He pointed toward the mountains. "They're something, ain't they? I never seen harder-looking mountains. The Smokies are prettier, ain't they, Lewis?"

"I wouldn't know."

"Yeah, they're prettier. The Smokies roll soft and pretty as a woman. These are hard mountains."

Lewis felt Elbridge's eyes burning into him. He turned and looked at him. "I'm sorry about your family," he said.

"I'll be with them soon. Soon as I get the message. Where's your family?"

"I never had any."

"Where you from? You talk like you come from the South."

"I fell off the moon."

"Really, you talk like the people I worked for. Back in North Carolina where I was cropping tobacco."

"You worked tobacco?"

"Man, did I work it. From planting season till market time. That's how I met Rita. You know tobacco?"

"A little. I know a little."

Elbridge slapped his leg. "I knew you were from the South. Ain't it something, Lewis? Me and you together this far from home." He looked out to the mountains. "I never worked harder, and I never lived better. The babies were cuter than buttons. I'd come in the house from work and smell butter beans and ham cooking. Rita always had a big pitcher of sweet tea in the refrigerator. Me and her would sit on the steps where it was cool and watch the sun set across the field. I hope heaven is like that. That was all I ever wanted."

Elbridge talked on, about the farm where he and Rita had lived, their garden out back, the chickens they had raised, the smell of the rain on late summer afternoons, and about hunting doves in the cut cornfields after Labor Day.

"It was something—money growing right out of the ground. But imagine, Lewis, me and you, standing here together after all these miles."

"I remember the summer I turned fifteen," Lewis said. "I was with this farmer I worked tobacco for. We were checking a barn that was being fired. A couple of sticks hadn't been hung right, and they'd fallen on the burners. They were scorched black, smoking. Another few minutes, they'd have been in flames, would have burned the whole barn down. We threw them outside. Carter stood there and looked at the barn, and then at them smoking leaves. I remember him saying, 'Fire's a funny thing, ain't it, boy? It'll cure tobacco or scorch it up in the field. It'll cook your food or burn your house down.' He said fire was a lot like life. 'You have to tend it all the time, all the parts. You study one part too long, another part might start to go out of control—or maybe just go out.' At the time, I didn't realize how right he was."

Elbridge pushed out his bottom lip. "I don't know, Lewis. When I saw them mountains from the other side, I thought all I had to do was come over them, and the whole world would make sense. I ain't so sure now." He pointed at a robin pecking at the ground beside the dumpster. "I always liked hunting birds. Mostly doves. I want to stand in a field and see the doves fly over."

"You're not going to see any doves around here."

"I used to love to hunt doves. You ever do any hunting?"

Lewis shook his head and shut his eye.

"Just past sunrise, and the birds are flying, and it's like you lock souls with 'em. They've fed me many a good meal, they could carry me straight to heaven. Ain't there a song about on the wings of a dove?"

Lewis wondered about this man, small as a boy, who believed in goodness and trusted birds to carry him to heaven. He turned his back to the mountain wall and went inside.

Elbridge

MIDNIGHT HAD PASSED, and the ward was dark and quiet, except for someone coughing or talking now and then in their sleep. I could hear the chugging sound of a respirator from some poor fellow's bed. A tube down his throat and one up his dick—all he could do was lay there and stare at the ceiling and wait to die. I never once seen a guy come off a respirator.

My faith was slipping. Everyone around me was hurting, and the air was thick with their body odors. The farm where me and Rita had our girls now seemed like heaven. I'd take it for heaven.

The social worker had been by that afternoon. She asked me if I had a will and, if I was to die, what I wanted done with my remains. I told her about the graveyard where my family was buried. She didn't say nothing, and I doubted they would send a body all that way for free.

I stared into the black ceiling, and for the first time since the fire, I was scared. I'm ashamed to admit it, but I kept hearing this little voice in the back of my mind that said I was going to lay there and hurt and die and be put in some puny grave, and there would never be a message or answer for me. I had come all this way on faith, but the only message I'd heard so far was the one from my own mouth.

Lewis

LEWIS WAITED on the balcony for the garbage man. He came at about the same time as the day before, again lugging a full load of scraps. He repeated the dumping process, and the rats scurried to the food as soon as he left. And just as it had the day before, the hawk arrived, picked up its prey, and shrieked and flew off. The feeding and fighting resumed on the ground below. Lewis shook his head, felt anger.

Patients at Friends' Hospital had to follow certain rules to be allowed to remain there. No drinking or smoking indoors, no fighting. They were not to demand too much of the medical staff, and those patients who were fit enough to be permitted to leave the hospital during the day had to return by six in the evening. Everyone who could get out of bed had a chore to do, mopping or sweeping or helping serve food. Lewis did what he was asked, and kept to himself. In a week, he figured, he would be strong enough to walk high into the mountains and lie down in the snow.

He was sweeping the kitchen pantry the next morning when, behind some large cans of food, he found a trap holding the carcass of a dead rat, dotted with maggots. He lifted the trap carefully and dropped it into a paper sack, then carried the sack to the bathroom and flushed the rat down the toilet. When he had finished sweeping, he washed the trap with soap and water, and brought it out to the dumpster. He pushed the trap stake into the dirt and set the trap, baiting it with a piece of toast. He went to the balcony to wait, and after a few minutes heard the door open behind him. Elbridge, who had spent all night and the morning sucking from an oxygen mask, shuffled over.

"You waiting on the hawk, Lewis? It only comes after lunch."

"I'm waiting on a rat."

"The rats don't come out except after the man brings the slop."

"We'll see."

A single rat appeared from below the dumpster, its nose twitching at the smell of food. Lewis pointed as more rats emerged. The first rat bolted forward to the food, and the trap snapped shut even quicker and tighter than the hawk's talons.

Elbridge stared wide-eyed at Lewis. "Why'd you do that?"

"That rat broke the rule. He shouldn't have done it."

"Rats don't understand traps. He didn't know there was a rule."

"Do any of us know the rules? The real ones?"

"I . . . I'm not so sure now. I used to think I knew the rules. The Ten Commandments."

Lewis laughed harshly. "Shit," he said.

"Ever since I got saved, I thought a man had to live by the Commandments. This last week, I started wondering. . . ."

Lewis turned away from Elbridge's words. He went to the dumpster below, pulled the near-dead rat from the trap, and hid both of them in a patch of weeds.

*

After lunch, Lewis watched the activity from the balcony. Once the rats—and the hawk—had feasted and left, he retrieved the trap and the dead rat from the weeds. He staked the trap and set it with the rat as bait.

How greedy are you? Lewis thought, searching the sky. Are you greedy too?

He had been on the balcony for nearly an hour when he saw the shadow. The hawk swooped down, talons spread wide to snatch the rat. Instead, the claws hit the trip plate, and the steel jaws clamped around both the hawk's legs, cutting to the bone.

Lewis thrust his arms aloft and cheered. Several patients heard him, and stared at him through the windows, but none dared come outside. On the ground below, the hawk shrieked and flapped its wings and tried time and again to rise; as much as it struggled, the trap chain held the creature to earth. Eventually its energy seemed to wane; the bird panted, sat with wings spread and quivering throughout the afternoon. Lewis stayed on the balcony the whole time, leaning against the railing and waiting for twilight to swallow the hawk.

He awoke with a start at dawn. The room was silent except for the snores of other patients. Lewis slipped from bed and went to the balcony. Only a pile of feathers and bones lay near the dumpster; the flesh of the great bird had been devoured. A few rats crawled over the remains, searching for stray shreds of meat.

Suddenly the air was rent by a flapping of wings, and another hawk swooped in. The bird clawed one of the rats, and as its predecessor had done, shrieked and flew away. Lewis watched until it became a spot against the eastern sky. He understood now.

*

Elbridge lay on his back, wearing his oxygen mask. He sat up when Lewis returned, and removed the mask. "Where'd you go?" he asked.

Lewis smiled. He told Elbridge what he'd done. "The hawk got eaten up. The rats came out and stripped him to the bone."

"Why do you like that, Lewis? The hawk was just being a hawk."

"Yeah, and he got greedy. Just like the rat. He didn't need another rat. You get greedy, you'll lose it all. Doesn't matter anyway. There's always another hawk waiting."

"What did you lose? Why don't you tell me?"

Lewis took a long breath. For a moment he feared he might cry. He sat down in a chair by Elbridge's bed and began his story.

"Greed did it," Lewis said when he'd revealed as much as he could. "Way back that first day, when my old man gave me that rifle, he said not to kill anything I didn't need. I didn't need that buck. The freezer was full of venison. Just my pride needed it. I spent my whole damn life having to prove to myself that I was as good as other people. I didn't need that buck. I didn't need to keep proving myself.

"There's a bunch of things: If I'd just let that deer go. If I hadn't stopped by Johnny's. Hell, I haven't ever been a liquor drinker. But I had to be a tough guy and take a challenge. If I hadn't fired that homeless guy . . .

"I should have listened to Bev. When that gun went off, she opened her mouth, and in a split second it was like she said a million words, and every one of them was true. I realized what I'd made myself into.

"Since the accident, I've believed that God was punishing me, but I don't anymore. There ain't no God. There's just rats and hawks, and they're both going to die, and be eaten or rot. There's only nature."

"But you set a trap, Lewis. That ain't nature."

"It's all a trap, but we do it to ourselves. There's no God. He couldn't be that mean."

Elbridge leaned toward Lewis and touched his scarred face. "What have you felt this last year? What have you felt?"

"What the hell do you think?"

"How did you feel before the accident?"

"I had a good life."

"Don't you see? Me and you, we've felt everything there is to feel, from A to Z. You've seen those people shopping at Pike Place. Most of them are just going through the motions of living. They try to feel as little as possible. Man, we know it all, from pain to love. All of it!"

Lewis shook his head. "I don't want to feel anymore. I've been waiting on God to kill me, and there ain't no God. I should have shot myself that morning beside the river."

Elbridge clasped Lewis's hand, then blinked hard. "Them doctors, they say I might start bleeding in my lungs any minute. But you're strong, you're going to live and understand all this. You got a little girl to go back to, a life."

"I can't go back."

"I been wrong about some things, Lewis. I can't change them now. There was a woman, and she needed me to hold her, and I turned from her. All she wanted was some love, and I had it locked up inside what I thought was a temple. I'm laying here dying now, and I'm afraid I ain't going to get no message. I ain't even going to know why that fire had to happen, and I come all this way. But you still got time, Lewis. You still got time to know."

Lewis stood. "No, it's time for me to end this. There are rats, and there are hawks, and I'd rather go out of this world as a hawk." He walked to his bed and lay facedown.

Early the next morning, Lewis put on his old street clothes, then packed his few belongings in his duffel. He stood over Elbridge and watched him labor through the oxygen mask. Maybe you'll go easy in your sleep, ol' boy, he thought. If there's something good out there, you deserve it. Maybe a flock of birds will swoop in here and carry you off.

He squeezed Elbridge's shoulder gently. "Remember, you were the one who went in the fire," he whispered. "You were the one."

Lewis walked to the hospital exit. He stepped out of the door and paused to gaze on Seattle. The air was cool, the downtown buildings dark against the blue water, the mountains sharp against the clear sky. He would head downtown, hoping he could make enough money for a bottle and bus fare to the mountains. Then he'd go into the woods, and lie down and drink until sleep came. He wouldn't think or feel or remember, and vermin would strip him and leave his bones for the earth, and at last he would be part of something clean and ordered and good.

The bums were beginning to stir at Pioneer Square and business people were converging on downtown.

Lewis saw a man lying wrapped in a blanket under his old oak tree, and under another tree the dog he had fed. He approached the animal, which lay on his side, eyes open but glazed over.

Lewis squatted beside the dog. "What happened, boy?" The dog thumped his tail. His front leg was swollen and red, and liquid oozed from a large wound. Lewis stroked the creature's head. "I'm sorry, fellow. You'll be better off soon. You won't have to hurt no more."

He placed his hands over the dog's nose and mouth, then tightened his grip. The dog barely struggled, and in less than half a minute went limp. Lewis stood and walked away.

At a street corner, he spotted a man in a suit waiting for a bus. Lewis walked up to him and tapped his arm. The man narrowed his eyes and stepped back.

"Mister," Lewis said, "I need twenty bucks. I know damn well you can spare it too."

The man reached into his jacket pocket. Without a word, he pulled out two tens from his wallet.

"Thanks," Lewis said, taking the money.

On his way to the liquor store, he saw the harelipped boy and a girl playing in the dirt yard in front of his house. Three men sat on the porch around a card table, playing poker and drinking beer.

The boy looked up as Lewis approached, and smiled. He glanced toward the porch, then spoke quietly. "Hi, Wuwis. Where you been?"

Lewis nodded. "Hey, boy." He was a few yards past the boy when he heard a voice from the porch.

"Hey, you little piss, what'd I tell you?"

Lewis swung his head around. The boy's father stood with his hands on his hips, his belly hanging over his belt. Lewis left the man shouting. His son walked toward him slowly with his head lowered.

A fifth of Popov in his duffel bag, Lewis started back toward Pioneer Square. As he neared the boy's house again, he saw only two men on the porch. From inside the house, he heard the wail of a child.

Lewis tried to shut his mind off from the world. He concentrated on an image of a landscape covered by snow, as soft and inviting as a down blanket. But the boy's cries pierced his skin and stabbed his ears, and grew only more shrill and high.

Lewis dropped his duffel bag and ran toward the house. One of the men on the porch stood in his way as he came up the steps. He shoved the man to the side, and the man went down backward. Lewis grasped the doorknob and swung the door open.

Across the front room stood the boy's father, one hand squeezing his son's arm, the other holding a lit cigarette. On the boy's chest were two fresh burns. The father dropped the cigarette and clenched his fist.

"You son of a bitch," Lewis shouted.

He met the man in the middle of the room, blocking his punch with a forearm, then slamming his face with a left and charging with his elbow into the man's gut. He held the man in a headlock and dragged him to the door. "You ain't so tough now, are you?" Lewis shouted.

The boy's father struggled to fight, but Lewis tightened his grip and clasped his hand over his mouth to muffle his curses. Out the front door they went, down the steps and toward the street. The two men on the porch moved away and watched; a few neighbors stared at the commotion.

"Get a cop," Lewis yelled. "Somebody call a cop."

On the sidewalk, he shoved the man to the concrete. When he crouched down and put his knee against the man's chest, the man responded by hammering against Lewis's leg.

"This guy is crazy," the boy's father shouted. "Get him off me."

The struggle continued, and a crowd gathered. No one tried to intervene, until finally a policeman appeared.

"What's going on here?" he demanded.

"This guy tried to kill me," the boy's father answered. "He's crazy."

The policeman reached for his billy club and looked at Lewis, who pushed his knee again into the man's chest, then stood. "He was burning his kid with a cigarette," he told the policeman. "Go look inside."

The boy's father coughed and spit as he rose to his feet. "This guy's a lunatic. Look at him!"

"He was burning the kid with a cigarette. I saw him. He's done it before. Just look at the kid's chest."

One of the men who had been playing cards spoke up. "Hey, cop, that guy attacked us. We were just standing there and he attacked us."

The policeman approached Lewis. "Sir, do you have some ID? I need to see it."

Lewis looked at the crowd of people and moved away from the policeman. "I haven't done anything wrong. You don't understand. He was hurting the kid."

"Arrest that freak!" the boy's father shouted. "He was trying to kill me."

"Sir, I need to see some ID right now," the policeman repeated. "Right now, or you're going downtown."

"But you don't understand," Lewis pleaded. "Just let me explain."

The policeman took his radio from his belt. "I need some backup," he said into the mouthpiece.

Lewis took another step away, then turned and ran. As he picked up his duffel bag and sprinted down the street, he could hear the policeman yelling for him to stop. He made it to an alleyway, where he paused to catch his breath. No one was following, and it was a quick walk to the park and the Salvation Army clothes bin.

There in the soft darkness, he lay like another thing discarded. He tried to block out his thoughts, but his blood was cleansed of alcohol, and his mind was sharp on the world. He reached into his duffel bag for the bottle of vodka. But something was in the way: the sight of the harelipped boy, walking head-down toward a man who, he knew, would burn him.

Lewis's tears came slowly, painfully, from deep inside. His chest heaved and his throat knotted as he tried to hold the tears back. They spilled down his cheek and dripped off his chin, washing from within him clods of dirt, rust, shards of glass. He cried for Beverly and for Lillian, but most of all, he cried for himself.

It was afternoon when Lewis awoke. He propped open the door to the bin and removed his ragged clothes, and searched through the pile until he found a shirt that fit and a pair of loose but clean trousers. He crawled out of the bin with his duffel bag and started toward the hospital on the hill.

Lewis entered Friends' without difficulty; no one asked where he had been all day. In the silence of the ward, he stood by Elbridge's bed and watched his long, labored breaths. A meal sat untouched on a table.

Lewis leaned over and shook the little man's shoulder. "Elbridge, wake up. You need to eat some soup."

Elbridge mumbled, but hardly stirred.

Lewis leaned again and whispered in his ear. "Elbridge, it's me, Lewis. You need to wake up and eat."

Elbridge fluttered his eyes open, then smiled weakly. "Lewis, I had a dream."

"Eat some of this soup." Lewis held the spoon to his mouth.

Elbridge shook his head. "I can't eat. Let me tell you about my dream."

"Tell me."

"I dreamed about mountains again. I walked up to this big mountain range, and you know what I did?"

"What'd you do?"

"I just stepped over it. I lifted my leg and stepped right over the top of the whole thing."

"That's good."

"Those mountains were high as the clouds, and I stepped right over the top of them." A smile spread on Elbridge's face before his eyelids lowered and he dropped back to sleep.

Lewis lay in bed in the dark, not sleeping. He heard Elbridge now and then mumbling about wheels, circles, turning, spinning. Around midnight, he started a coughing spasm. He rolled onto his side, hacked and spit and gasped for breath.

"Go ahead and die, dammit," came a voice from across the room. "Just let me sleep."

"Yeah, shut up, motherfucker," another voice called.

Lewis rose from his bed. "I hear another word, I'll break your damn necks!" he thundered. He walked to

Elbridge's bed. "What can I get for you? What do you need?"

Elbridge strained to speak. "I been wrong about the whole thing. There ain't no message for me. There wasn't any reason for the whole thing."

Lewis put his hands under Elbridge's shoulders. "No, you were right. There *was* a reason for our coming here. I'm still not sure what it is, but you were right."

"No. I don't think so anymore. All Rita ever wanted me to do was love her, and I turned away. I did it to Kathy too." Elbridge coughed again and again, and blood bubbled from his mouth.

Why didn't anyone come to help the guy? Lewis wondered. He went to the nurses' station and banged his fist on the counter.

"Can't you hear him in there? He needs help. Get someone now!" he demanded.

The nurse pushed a button on the wall, then hurried to Elbridge's bedside and took his pulse. A sleepy-looking doctor arrived a moment later. The doctor pulled painkiller from a vial into a syringe and stuck a needle in Elbridge's arm. When his coughing had abated, the nurse and the doctor rolled him onto his back.

"He needs a ventilator," the nurse said.

"It won't do him any good," answered the doctor.

"He'll go easier."

The doctor sighed aloud. "Get it set up. I need to call in for authorization."

Lewis watched the two walk away. He thought of the air outside and the night sky filled with stars. He put on his boots and took the blanket from his bed. With his duffel over one shoulder, he went to Elbridge's bedside, draped the blanket over him, and lifted the small man into his arms. Lewis scanned the room for a nurse, then moved quickly toward the rear of the ward, and the exit beyond. He pushed the door open with his foot, setting off the alarm as he had feared. And then, the bell clanging behind him, he ran carrying Elbridge into the moon-drenched night.

Lewis felt arms surrounding him. He opened his eye to see the shimmer of the aurora borealis, rolling through the heavens like a great wave. The lights merged, and when they did, he saw a form take shape. Her hair and gown undulating with the light. Her voice as gentle as the wind in the tree boughs . . .

Who is saved and who is the savior, love? One may not exist without the other. If I were able to heal your scars and return you to a day in the past, I would harm you worse with such a gift of ignorance. Search your heart now for what you know to be true and what you know to be false; your gift has visited few in flesh.

As spirit I have the secrets of time and stars. When I was human, I did not know that joy is best sweetened by pain, jubilation by heartache. Yet you possess this gift while you breathe, your knowledge born not of the burden you carried upright and strong, but of the weight that crippled you.

Salvation is as simple as the seed. Fruit blooms from year to year, into the eons, the child of every seed. What of our child? A heart as tempered as yours can no longer deny her. She is still pure of heart, a blank page waiting for the words. She is redemption, our own denial not visited upon our young. Who better to teach her the words than one whose heart has survived fire? Teach her your lessons of pain, and may she grow to never keep her words within walls of flesh. Hold her and you hold me. She is our forgiveness, her innocence is without boundaries.

Look into the sky, love. Lest you forget the long path, with my finger I will point the way.

The meteor slipped from the heavens and streaked eastward. By the time it was over the two men, its head was blue-hot, and a long plume trailed behind. The fireball slid faster toward the mountains; it would mesh flame and stone in some desert plain beyond. For minutes after the meteor had passed, a vapor trail remained, luminous. Lewis searched the sky above, but fantasy or fact, *her* form had disappeared.

Like a laser, the meteor opened a door for Lewis through the mountain wall, and the morning came all at once. He unwrapped the blanket and shook his companion gently.

"The birds are coming, Elbridge. Wake up. The doves will be here soon."

"Doves . . . doves." Elbridge blinked up at the man who held him. "Lewis, that you? Where are we?"

"We're at the cornfield. It's opening day, the doves will be coming in soon."

"There ain't no doves coming."

"You're wrong. The doves are going to fly."

Elbridge's head fell back against Lewis's chest, as if he were melting into his skin. Lewis watched the pulse on the side of the man's neck, a few steady beats, then a pause, more beats, and another pause.

Lewis spoke softly. "We both went in that fire, didn't we? You know we did. You went in it, and I went in it, and we got burned bad. We went in, but we came out. There ain't many people who can claim that, are there? Not many. We can't blame ourselves for coming out. Not when we had to go in. We can't blame ourselves no more."

Elbridge tried to lift his head and speak. "I been dreaming the craziest dreams, Lewis. I can't explain them. They're not bad dreams." He paused, fought for breath. "You know what?"

"What?"

"I'm a half-breed nigger with orange hair."

"You ain't no nigger."

"Yeah, I am. And it don't matter. Names don't mean a thing. You know what else?"

"What?"

"I'm from the tribe of humans. That's my tribe."

"Mine too, Elbridge."

A ray of sunlight glinted gold from behind the mountains. Lewis looked above, and from side to side. He pointed to the sky. "See that dove coming over those spruces?"

Elbridge tilted his head. "I can't see too good."

"A dove just flew right over us. Right over us, Elbridge. And here come two more. They're flying!" Again Elbridge tilted his head toward where Lewis pointed. "My eyes ain't too good."

"Opening day, Elbridge. The doves are coming into the cornfield to feed. Look—three more from over that same tree. Right at us. If we had a shotgun we could knock 'em down."

A smile spread slowly over Elbridge's face, and he leaned closer to Lewis. "Yeah, I can see 'em," he said weakly. "I see 'em now. They're coming over the tree-tops like manna from heaven. They wing on. I'd just let them fly."

Lewis felt the little man heavier and heavier against him. "They're thick as flies," he said. "I never saw so many doves. It's a feast."

Elbridge's chest rose quick and high, and he exhaled in a long whisper. His head rolled to one side against Lewis's shoulder.

Lewis extended his bad hand as if sighting down a gun barrel, and fired, "Pow, pow, pow." He shifted his gaze from the sky to Elbridge's face—his eyes were closed, his lips slightly apart, the breeze tousled his hair. "I love you, buddy," he said.

He rocked his friend back and forth until the sun had climbed high above the wall.

Lewis laid Elbridge down in the shade of a spruce tree; he cushioned his head with the blanket and folded his hands across his chest. Back at the rock, he pulled the fifth of vodka from his duffel bag. He turned to the east, raised the bottle, and poured a steady stream of liquor on his scalp. The cold liquid ran down his face and dripped onto his shoulders and chest. He threw the empty bottle into the nearby woods, then sat down against the rock. The young sun would dry him and warm him while he slept.

A late sun was tracing its golden path across Puget Sound when Lewis stood up from the rock: earth and time were turning in their endless circles. Lewis walked toward the mountains slowly, until darkness began to engulf him. Child to savior: Lewis now knew that sometimes a man had to come to the end to find his beginning.

Ahead of him the streetlights of a town shone larger and brighter. Lewis approached a lone telephone booth on the side of the road and paused in front of it. He stared at his reflection in the glass, and in that dimness saw a man he once knew, with large, capable hands and brown eyes that glittered.

From the back of his mind, he recalled a face and a phone number. The door of the phone booth cried like a child as he opened it and raised his hand toward life.